THE WIZARD TIM

By Tim Allen

Mundus butyri et saccharo

The Wizard Tim by Tim Allen

First Printed Edition

ISBN: 979-8-9869108-3-3

Book Cover by Peyeyo
X: @peyeyoillustrates
Instagram: @peyeyoilustrador

Edited by Kristie LaMantia (@paralledit)

Published by Sugarpig Productions Inc.
wizardtim.com

Acknowledgements

I'll begin by calling out the fact that this book was never originally intended to be minted as an NFT. Truth be told, this book wasn't originally written to even be read by the public. In fact, the stories of a fat wizard named Tim were purely written to poke fun at a college best friend who one day got high and said he felt like a wizard… that was clearly a mistake.

I'd like to also mention that ninety-five percent of this book was written by Joseph Eleam. So, first and foremost, the biggest credit must be given to the extraordinary wit that seems to exist within that balding head of his. The unending stream of potty humor, innuendos, and other foul things that pour out of his brain never ceases to amaze me. My hope is (as it has always been) that our publishing this book provides some modicum of confidence to this southern gentleman—who was once "blinded by the bright lights of Auburn"—so that he is encouraged to give the world access to his creativity long into the future.

My contribution, while maybe less heavy on the writing (except for Randall's song and the unfortunate encounter Tim has with

4

a female ogre in chapter twenty; those were all me, as Joe will gladly be the first to tell you), was a significant one nonetheless. My role was largely in the task of taking this mountain of sycophantic, unrefined literary gold and turning it into something that people would consider reading. To that end, I turned to the community that I had personally been welcomed by and grown to love: the Cardano community.

To Charles Hoskinson: In the unlikely event that you may read this, I would like to thank you for your creation of Cardano. While you may not have known the full gravity of your creation at the time, I am sure you are delighted to see that it has since become a spawning ground for unlikely friendships and creative growth. The idea of publishing a book as a pair of part-time authors with other responsibilities and no chance of having enough time to try and get picked up by a major publisher was discouraging to say the least. However, the concepts of true ownership, enforceable identity, and unfiltered open environments have led to the reality that anyone can publish something if they want. That reality, paired with a community that respects and seeks out new ideas and creators, made the dream of publishing this novel about a fat wizard seem achievable. Now, in the even more unlikely event that you choose to read this book after reading these acknowledgments, I hope the community can forgive us for polluting your brain.

To Paul Jenkins: The only actually qualified person to have heard the concept of this book before it was published in any form. Thank you for not shutting us down, and in fact encouraging us to go for it. Your willingness to give audience and feedback to unknown creators like us, while at your level, is amazingly charitable. I know you take pride in helping burgeoning writers, and I hope that this book helps contribute in a positive way to that pride — or is at least a neutral contribution.

To Our Families: We are sorry.

To Paralledit: The only actual magic that exists in this book is what you did to fix it. If it wasn't for your painstaking eye for detail, and unbelievable immunity to ridiculously stupid things, we'd be lost. We were beyond lucky to find you.

To the Book.io Community: This book, in this format, would not have happened without you. The support you showed to us when we sold an early, unedited, and extremely crude version of it is, frankly, absurd. You are all degenerates, and we love you.

Lastly, to Our Readers: It is highly recommended that you enjoy this book while sitting in a comfy seat, smoking your finest herb, and eating a slice, or five, of pie. There may be times that this book confuses you, disgusts you, or possibly even arouses you. In the event you feel any of these sensations, be sure to take another puff of herb and eat another bite of pie. You'll be fine. It's just a book. Good luck.

Thanks for reading,
Tim Canada

Author's Note:

I mostly agree with the above,
Joseph Eleam

*You may be inclined to think that this page was intention-
ally left blank to ensure the book begins on an even page.*

*However, it was actually left blank because I, Tim, the
formatter of this book, do not wish to update the layout of
all following pages by updating this error.*

It is on this note of apathy, that we begin.

Enjoy with pie.

Prologue

*T*his is a story about a wizard. Now, as most understand it, wizards should be smart, brave, and possess the sage-like knowledge that only time and long life can bestow. While this is true for most wizards, the wizard in this particular tale does not happen to be blessed with any of these particular traits.

This wizard's name is Tim.

Tim holds the position of town wizard to a cozy halfling village named Halfass. Halfass is widely regarded by its residents as the most boring village in the world; and while many might say this of their own hometown, very few have the records to support such claims. However, Halfass has not had a recorded crime, disaster, or even notable event in its entire recorded existence, which by current accounts happens to be just over five hundred years.

Of course, as the resident town wizard, Tim claims full credit for maintaining such a stellar record of uneventfulness, but he silently retained the truth… that he had done absolutely nothing at all. In fact, the truth is that this dull setting of Halfass allowed Tim to be as lazy as he wanted to be.

You see, the thing to understand about Tim is that while he is an actual wizard who graduated from wizarding school like all the rest, he very much prefers reading about adventure and magic over actually practicing it. So, the position of town wizard in a boring town like Halfass is an absolute dream for a wizard like Tim.

The post includes many perks like retirement, monthly salary, a travel stipend, and one of the coziest holes in the entire village, which Tim has grown so fond of that he even named it. It's a well-known tradition among the Half-folk to name your own hole and to make sure it has deep and personal meaning. Like any wizard would do, Tim thought long and hard of a name that would suit. As Tim first walked the hallowed grounds of his moist home, admiring the finely ribbed walls, he could think of no one else. Back at wizarding school, there had been a forbidden, unrequited love, a love that led to a fetish that he now often enjoyed. The warmth and tight spacing of the hole reminded him of the majestic creature that had been his professor of Intro to Beastiality, who introduced him to the wide world of beasts, men, and things they could put in interesting places. Her name was Kim, and thus, so became the name of his dwelling hole.

Thank you, Professor Kim.

Tim has done everything he can to turn Kim into the pure definition of comfort. In each corner of every room, Tim has taken great care to procure the most comfortable seats that the space would allow in which to sit, relax, read, and gently drift off into a nap.

Now, while Tim loves to nap, his favorite hobby happens to be eating.

Eating is serious business to Tim, and while it was already a specialty of the halfling folk that resided in Halfass, it was not long after Tim arrived that even they came to respect and fear the wizard's appetite. Tim would often scour the village farms for tasty treats and even hired a local halfling named Julie to help him ferret out all the sweetest delicacies from around the kingdom and beyond.

In fact, Tim's most prized possession happens to be the book of recipes that he has painstakingly collected and perfected over the course of his entire career as the town's wizard. He would often sit in his comfy seats and read over the recipes critically, barking orders at Julie to cook whichever ones caught his fancy at any given moment.

Needless to say, the combination of Tim's simple post, paired with his lazy hobbies, has led him to cultivate a certain… erm… size.

To put it all very plainly, Tim has found himself the absolute best life a lazy, obese wizard could ever dream of, and it is here that our story begins, on an ordinary pie Tuesday, with Tim nuzzled deep in one of the coziest seats in his hole, Kim.

*T*im woke to the sound of malformed feet and dirty, filling-covered hands attempting to open his door. He had been three hours deep into his morning nap; it was nearing what some would consider a sleep, and yet as the filling-doused fingers neared his knob, he came awake with a start. He thought about kicking himself for nearly missing his favorite weekly activity, the great pie delivery.

Tim told his mind to leap out of his favorite armchair, only to find that the command to leap would no longer move him very much. All he succeeded in doing was creating a small gush of some sort of fluid somewhere he could not see or touch easily. Shrugging, he reached for his mighty wizard's staff, slammed it into the wood flooring, and used it to slowly lift his considerable bulk from the chair.

Passing by the mirror on the way to the door, he discovered a little surprise to brighten his mid-morning mood. It seemed that in his haste to take a proper nap, Tim had left half a cookie in the gnarled, greasy ropes of his beard. He plucked the offering out with his finger and popped it into his mouth.

"That wasn't a cookie," he mumbled to no one in particular as he swallowed the mystery snack.

With an extra spring in his step, Tim swiftly moved to answer the door, trying desperately to ignore the back pain that the extra spring had caused him. As he swung open the large wooden door of Kim, he was delighted to see one of his favorite sights: his personal halfling attaché, Julie, holding two armfuls of tasty pies.

"Julie, where did you get these pies?"
"I found them, Tim," Julie said, looking at his feet.
"Found them? What, in the street?"
"No, under a bush."
"There's only one type of bush that you find pies under, Julie, and they don't look like that."

Julie looked as many halflings did, half the size of a man while standing on his tiptoes and equally as wide. His habit of eating as much as a pair of sows daily made him look like a walking orb with a few stunted limbs jutting off at mostly the correct places. Like most halflings, the thick hair that covered most of his body and head gave him the appearance of some sort of out-of-control beaver or platypus. Most everything about him was typical for a halfling, except for the great shocks of blonde hair that covered the little monster's feet. Tim knew he was actually quite proud of this for some reason.

Julie glanced about nervously, suggesting this particular batch of pies was indeed stolen, or maybe a local sheep had gone missing... again.

"Well, Julie my lad, it seems you've truly outdone yourself this time!" Tim exclaimed, once again ignoring all the warning signs.

Julie was not the brightest of halflings. However, Tim had

found him to be quite industrious while ferreting out the tastiest treats this side of Halfass and beyond. Julie had an affinity for the sweet dishes of the lands and had on occasion traveled great distances to procure a particularly tasty-sounding dish, though only half of his bundles seemed to make it all the way back to Tim's halfling hole, Kim.

This, perhaps, was the trait that made Tim like Julie so much. For while Tim was often quite hard on Julie, their mutual love of food sometimes led him to believe they were kindred spirits. Each looked at the other as sort of a dimwitted pet that they were forced to tolerate, and the fact that Julie was willing to steal for his own enjoyment made Tim never feel bad when he did the exact same thing to him.

As Tim looked over his servant's discoveries, he could already feel his salivary glands moisten.

"As you know, m'lord, I take nothing more serious than our comfort and foodings," said Julie.

Tim did know this.

"Julie, my dear, come and sit on my knee and tell me of all these wonderful delicacies you've brought to me today," responded Tim.

"Well, m'lord, today we have quite the assortment you'll be pleased to hear. We have a mix of your standard berry pies: blueberry, raspberry, strawberry, boysenberry, and the like. Plus, not too bad of a selection of tarts either, m'lord. I think you'll be particularly fond of the peach one. The locals spoke very highly of it, so I went ahead and procured the recipe for your book as well."

Julie began to take out the intricately etched recipe book from the leather pack on his back. Of all the possessions in Kim's hole, there were none that Tim prized more than his precious recipe book. It contained all the best and most wonderful treats that Tim had ever tasted. Tim had Julie keep them all safely recorded on the nicest paper that could be found so that they could be easily reproduced whenever Tim felt one of them calling to him.

"Excellent! Excellent!" Tim half moaned with delight as he rubbed his greasy palms together. "But my Julie, which will we try first?!"

With this question, Tim noticed that Julie's face had suddenly become overwhelmed with a somber expression.

"What is it, Julie? Is your gut giving you the hot snakes again?"

Julie looked down; he did not like to be reminded of that particular bathroom incident, and his master knew that.

"No sire, I fear it's worse than any restroom demon. I'm afraid it's… it's work," said Julie in a depressed tone.

"**W**ork?!? What in the name of sourdough could they possibly need me to do?" shouted Tim.

Julie extended a short scroll to his master. Tim, of course, first grabbed one of the pies and stuffed it down his gullet, which made him even more upset because he had swallowed the thing whole and didn't even get a taste of the filling, but then after he had finished consoling himself with a second treat, he finally examined the short scroll that Julie had handed to him.

Licking clean the sugary jam from his own fingers, as he unrolled the scroll, he noticed in the tight rolling scrawl of half-man script that there were at least two smudges of unidentified jams that were quite clearly different from the jam he was presently eating.

"Julie?" said Tim accusingly, like a master to a dog.

Julie looked down at his feet. He couldn't see them, but he knew they were there, probably.

"Did you read my correspondence from Sir Wrinkly Pog?" he asked.

"I just wanted to make sure, err, to make positive, master was not in trouble for any strange happenings," replied Julie.

"Strange happenings? What do you mean, Julie?" Tim asked with a tentative caution.

"Nothing too serious sir, murders, robberies and the like, ya know… kid stuff," muttered Julie in an oddly calm tone that did not match the seriousness of the topics he mentioned.

"Very well…"

Tim was slightly annoyed at this mistake in decorum; also, as usual, Julie's wording was… bizarre…

With a belch, he began to read the letter aloud:

> *"To our noble protector:*
>
> *Tim, it is with due haste I request your presence at the town hall. A matter most urgent.*
>
> *Yours Truly,*
> *Sir Wrinkly Pog"*

As Julie unloaded the wagon with the greatest of care, Tim took to his chambers to make himself as presentable as possible. Julie knew that this would likely take some time, so he took the opportunity to slink off with a few of the pies down into his most secret of hideouts.

It was not very often that Tim was called to the King's Hall on actual business; he usually made his rounds during holidays, festivals, and any occasion for a feast, of course. Tim greedily rubbed his fingers together as he imagined the festival of delights that must await him as they have on all the other occasions he had traveled to the hall. Digging through his trunk, he found his largest and least dirty robe. Setting it aside for a few moments, he polished his staff several times for good luck and spun three times afterwards but neglected to wash his hands following the acts. Then, as he put on the robe, he noticed a fresh stain on his undershirt but decided to ignore it. It was directly over his belly button. Surely no one would notice, he thought to himself.

He then grabbed his unpolished staff from the hallway and was mostly satisfied with his outfit. For a bit of decoration, he wore his pie-eating medal from last year's harvest festival and hoped the sight of it would instill a bit of jealousy in the old eyes of Sir Pog.

As Tim continued to fuss over himself, trying to make himself look less like a water-swollen hog with love-stained attire, Julie used the time to crawl deeper and deeper into his special place.

It was dark and dirty, just like Julie liked it. He knew the way by heart and rarely had to light a torch unless one of his guests became too unruly. At last, he arrived in the section he wanted, and Julie plopped down with one of his pies and lit a small, wax candle.

"Mhmm, boysenberry," he mumbled as he dug around in the ancient pile of books before him.

Julie threw and scattered the books for several minutes before he found the one he was looking for, the great black one.

The large black book was Julie's favorite; it contained pictures of lots of dead things and bones, which he enjoyed quite a lot. However, no matter how many skulls he found on the outside, they never quite matched the book; they were always smaller than depicted.

Julie grimaced and turned towards the back once again. To his great despair, Julie discovered there was only one of the shiny pages left. With a heavy heart, he ripped the page out and carefully inscribed the peach tart recipe on the back. Taking out Tim's spell book, he licked the edge of the page and stuck it in the back. It stuck inside the book like glue. That was one advantage to uncontrolled type II diabetes, Julie guessed.

From above, Julie could hear Tim's ponderous gait, and as quick as a shadow, he left his subterranean refuge.

"Come along, Julie. We haven't got all day!" shouted Tim, the bellow ringing throughout Julie's secret halls.

Julie moaned something unintelligible in reply that sounded like an affirmative. Tim didn't look at him as he strode past, and Julie felt his feelings take a small hit. Julie then wiped a mixture of boysenberry jam and dirt from his face and did a sort of loping roll to catch up with his master.

Tim and Julie started the climb down the hill from Tim's great hole and were greeted as they passed through the streets of Halfass. Tim loved to see the people going about their days — the bakers baking, the brewers brewing, the… bakers baking. He was actually quite distracted by the bakers baking and very strongly considered stopping by and having a taste, but it was not like Sir Pog to send him a summons that wasn't a social invitation.

However, in all his decades of protecting Halfass as their official wizard, he had never actually needed to do any protecting, so whatever the issue was, he doubted it would require… well… any real work at all.

The king of Halfass would be more akin to a lord in a large human settlement, but the Halflings were long-lived and did not overly breed, so their kingdom was small but proud.

The keep was the largest structure in the town and was almost defensible — not that the battlements had ever actually been manned. The town guard of Halfass consisted of several old drunks who spent more time eating and drinking than doing anything else, and as Tim and Julie climbed the short stone staircase, they saw one of the guards sleeping by the doorway. Tim poked the sleeping man with his foot, but he was simply shooed away, and Tim and Julie carried on.

"Tsk, tsk, why is it the laziest sods that get to enjoy the day, and the rest of us must work for a living?" Tim said in a condescending tone. Julie shrugged and a few crumbs fell out from his collar.

"Julie, I suppose you will have to announce me since the guard is having a bit of a sleep," said Tim.

Julie rolled his eyes but dutifully opened the large oak door and stepped inside. With a bellow, he announced:

"Your Majesty, may I present the protector of Halfass, the great pie eater, the cookie dunker, and the destroyer of cake holes, the sultan of swat himself. Your wizard, Tiiiiiiiiiiiiiiiiim!"

As Julie finished his announcement, Tim strode in and was surprised to find Sir Pog sitting at his long table, looking over a piece of paper. It being two o'clock in the afternoon, Tim had expected to ruin the ole boy's afternoon nap.

Sir Pog stood and ushered Tim over to the table.

"Tim, so good of you to come quickly. I know there are other things we have to discuss between ourselves; however, we might actually have a problem," said the halfling king in a concerned tone.

It was at this statement that Tim's blood began to run cold. Sir Pog had not mentioned his weight even once nor even given his pie-eating medal a glance, and he knew he was envious of it. Putting on an air of seriousness, Tim walked over quickly and took in the documents on the great table. Most of the table was taken up by a large map and a small handwritten note. In its center stood the village of Halfass, and it seemed the old fortifications were highlighted. The only thing Tim found more surprising than Pog looking at the defenses was the fact that the old dog could read at all!

Tim knew from experience that none of these fortifications had been maintained in his long tenure as town wizard, and he suspected it had been much longer than that. He walked up next to the king and very cavalierly showed off his pie-eating medal.

"The defenses, Sir Pog?" muttered Tim.

"Yes, a dimwitted serving boy was able to scrape these out of the cellar," said Sir Pog, stroking his beard.

"Why are you looking to defend the town's defense? There hasn't been so much as a wildcat spotted in the halfling territories for more than an age."

"Times are set to change Tim, as they often do. I have received troubling reports from abroad. The kingdoms of men, Elves, and Dwarves all say the dark beasts are out in the world again. I had assumed it was just the talk of warmongers, always looking for the next adventure, the next way to get a leg up on their neighbor…" Sir Pog replied.

Tim noted the tone of sadness in the old half-man's voice, and this caused a tinge of fear to run up the old wizard's spine. He even let the comment about getting a leg up on his neighbor go by without a smirk.

"What do you mean? Surely nothing too serious," Tim added a nervous laugh at the end to defuse the situation.

Sir Pog pointed to a distant farmhouse marked on the map and said,

"The Pumplekins' farm."

"Yes, I know them well," replied Tim.

Tim began to think of all the delicious melons he had tasted from the Pumplekins, the daughters Beatrice and Eveleen especially.

"They were all killed in an attack yesterday; the signs point to goblins. Not a half-man, woman, child, or beast made it out, though we did find pieces," Sir Pog said somberly.

With a gasp, Tim replied,

"Goblins? Here in Halfass? No, no, certainly not."

Sir Pog went on,

"A corpse was found in the farmyard; it looks as if old Pumplekin, or one of his sons, gutted one with a pitchfork. Halfling blood was everywhere, and the barn house burned to the ground. Several remains were found inside, thought to be that of his family and a few bits of the animals."

Tim sat down with a mighty plop.

"It doesn't make any sense, Pog! The green scourge and all their ilk were pushed out way beyond the borderlands. Week's journey from here. How could a goblin band make it all the way to the heartlands?" he said, exasperated.

Sir Pog replied in an assertive manner,

"I don't know, Tim, but you need to find out. You and your… erm… your creature here must set out at once. Find me something. I don't know if it was a roving band or a single goblin. Or something worse. Harvest day is set for the end of this week, and if we have to cancel the festival… I don't know what would become of us."

Tim was in shock; he had never thought, well certainly never expected, to actually have to be a wizard for Halfass. In fact, in the hundred years of him living in the town, the only time he had been called to help was when the king had gotten himself stuck in a butter tub.

Julie looked worriedly over his master; he had never seen him so upset — not since the great jam drought of 192 ED, but that was nothing like this. During the jam outage, Tim had simply wept and was forced to eat apple pie and cake in his underwear, often covered in tears and filth. But this, this was next-level despair.

*B*ack at his halfling hole, Kim, Tim was currently curled up on the floor being spoon-fed raspberry jam as his head rested on Julie's lap. Julie was twirling his hair between his jam-covered, stubby fingers.

"There, there, it will be alright, sir. Maybe we just go out, have a little picnic, and have a look about? Maybe the gobbies have already gone," whispered Julie.

This caused a thin globule of jam to drip out of Tim's mouth. He hadn't even considered that a possibility! With a jam-infused sniffle, he sat up and realized that if he just stuck to the letter of the request and went out and browsed around the farm, maybe had a quick picnic with Julie, and obviously ran if they happened to see anything suspicious, then the two could come back into town a little worse for the wear, having spent the night out of doors. Maybe he would rub a little mud to complement the food stains he knew would come about. They might even be treated as heroes! Yes, the wizard and his servant who spent the night OUTSIDE for the common good of Halfass; it might even get them a little sympathy from some of the fairer of the half-women around town. This plan at least seemed to give Tim a glimmer of hope that he could maintain his life of comfort and not be revealed as a total sham.

"You're right, Julie. Let us prepare for the picnic. A good meal and a walk in the woods doesn't sound so bad," he said with a renewed sense of energy.

"Yes, your err… wizardness. I will make us a meal that you probably won't forget," muttered Julie.

After all, they had done that hundreds of times. Some of those memories were better than others. Tim noted that about half of those picnics wound up with him missing several hours of his time and usually waking up to a shirtless Julie…

Tim decided to at least put on a proper adventure outfit while Julie made the other preparations.

Going through his magical trunk, Tim began to search. The trunk technically opened in another place entirely, one that, as far as Tim knew, was made exclusively to store items. He had never paid too much attention in his theoretical magical theory class and honestly did not find it very interesting but was very appreciative that it was cluttering that dimension and not his.

Leaning as deeply into the chest as he dared, Tim began to pull out items. He had many robes. A great many actually. Most had been stained with some sort of food or fluid throughout the years. The intention was to have them cleaned at some point, but this never actually seemed to happen. After an hour or so of sifting through his robes and flicking globs of dried crust from his fingers, Tim was starting to notice a trend about himself. Over time, his robes both increased in size and in their general level of filth. What could that possibly mean? His mind hovered on this unanswerable question only for an instant. Deep down, he knew the answer, but to fix all of his glaring issues would require willpower, a thing he had no interest in developing at this point in his life.

As he neared the bottom, he finally came across what he was looking for, his officially sanctioned wizard wear. Not that wizards had a uniform or anything; most matched magical pieces that they either created or acquired across a long and storied career. Maybe a wizard would make a chest piece from the hide of a magical beast that had attacked his town, or perhaps would be given a reward from a pleased king or famous artificer. Tim's outfit consisted of the robes he had left school with and some lightly enchanted leather armor.

Tim had not strapped on that outfit since the day he left the academy, and it took him and Julie the better part of an hour to get it to fit on him at all.

"A bit tight, but I feel good," Tim said as he tried to breathe through clenched teeth.

Julie wiped sweat from his pouring brow.

"Yes, boss, you look like a threefer' sausage in a one sausage skin, if I do say so myself!" Julie said exhaustingly.

Tim grabbed his staff and a short sword someone had given him long ago and made for the exit. He ignored the sausage comment and tried not to let Julie see the sadness it had caused on his face. Julie grabbed up an exceptionally large pack but then seemed to hesitate a bit at the threshold of the door.

"Julie?"

Tim asked as a father would to a hesitant child. Julie hesitated and looked down at his feet.

"What is it? We need to leave before it gets too dark, or we might not be able to even have a proper fire. Do you want to be cold and snuggling up to my backside?"

Julie was afraid of goblins, and he was worried some of the pies would turn if they weren't eaten on the way.

"Nothing, sir. Just worried about ourselves... and the pies o' course."

Tim just nodded, focusing on his own anxiety over the present situation. With the pair equally focused on their own fears, they grabbed their gear and set off for the road.

*I*t only took a very slow five minutes of walking for Tim and Julie to reach the outskirts of Halfass. Gravity, that bastard, continued to pull Tim down the hill out of town and on the worn-out drawstring that attempted to cinch his robe. The eastern road yawned out before them and extended into the darkening forest beyond. Tim hadn't been this close to a forest near dark in a long time, and all the sounds emanating from it truly terrified him. The sounds, sights, and smells of his dwelling hole, Kim, were his world now, and being outside of it truly felt alien to him. Tim noticed that Julie seemed quite anxious since he nervously looked over his shoulder at every sound they heard.

While they walked very close to a copse of large oaks, Julie stopped and put his dirty finger to Tim's lip.

"Hear things, master."

Julie's eyes did that thing they do, rolling around in his head and then straightening back up and looking more like a predator's. Tim tried to listen, but the only sound he could hear was the beating of his overworked heart. It thumped DIA… betes… DIA… betes… and on and on.

Tim crouched, and his body, betraying him once again, passed a foul wind that made Julie begin to cough and gag. After the spell had passed, Tim and Julie sat quietly on the road, and at last, Tim could hear something. A voice, no two. It was a conversation.

"I say, Redleaf, these squirrels sure are… nuts… lice."

The other voice answered.

"That's nothing compared to the wood… pecker… my nuts are… swollen."

Tim knew what this was.

"It's the damn trees, Julie. Talking of their nuts."

Julie shrugged. He did not talk to trees.

Tim did, but he preferred talking to maples rather than oaks. They were such gossips. The two slipped past without being dragged into conversation.

An hour after dark, the adventurous pair came to a small turn-off on the road. It was the turnoff to the Pumplekins' farm. Tim's heart began to race, and he absent-mindedly reached into his chest piece and pulled out a piece of cheese.

"One bite now, and one bite after we make it out of the farm," he whispered.

Tim looked behind him and saw Julie was doing something similar, except his courage seemed to consist of half a tin of cookies. Smart. Tim was envious and wondered if they were oatmeal or some sort of shortbread. Shaking his head, he remembered this was not the time for such thoughts; actual danger might lie ahead.

After walking down the well-used path for a minute, the two crept to the side of the road and dropped their packs.

"Julie, come here," whispered Tim.

"What?" replied Julie at his normal volume level, which was a bit of a scream.

"Shhhhh!" Tim shushed rather loudly.

"What?" Julie asked louder, not understanding what Tim was trying to express.

Feeling his anger come over him, Tim used his hand to cover Julie's mouth and bent down to whisper in his ear. Julie, once again misunderstanding the situation, began to frantically lick Tim's hand. Tim, repulsed by the licking, bellowed out a hearty,

"YUCK! and attempted to dry his hand on his pants while shrieking, "Julie, why did you do that?!"

Julie still did not understand what was going on. Why was Tim always so difficult? Sometimes, he wants him to lick his hand; tonight, he puts his cheese-smelling hand on his mouth, and when Julie very graciously licks it, Tim shrieks like a ghost.

"I thought you wanted me to guess the cheese again?" said Julie.

"Damn it, Julie, no. We are trying to be stealthy," retorted Tim.

"OOOOOOHHH," Julie said in his normal speaking tone.

Tim used his hands to motion to take the volume down, and the light finally went on in Julie's dimwitted face.

"I get it, sir," Julie said in a whisper.

Tim was getting to the point where he was beyond caring and thought a roughly hewn goblin spear through his heart—or perhaps Julie's—might not be so bad. With his knees loudly cracking, Tim bent down to Julie's level.

"What's the plan, Tim?" asked Julie. "I could use part of the flambé supplies to make us look more intimidating."

Tim shook his head and put his hands over his face.

"We have no idea what's out there, Julie. I think a stealthy approach would work best. Also, we don't want to be caught dead without our flambé supplies. This is a picnic after all," he replied.

Julie made no reaction and just stared blankly at Tim.

"You know… stealth? Being quiet?"

"Ahh yes, sneaky Julie," said Julie in a strangely experienced tone.

"Yes, sneaky. Can you do that?" asked Tim.

"Julie can be most sneaky. Yes, most sneaky indeed. Many hidden talents Julie has…"

Julie said this with a very concerning wink in his eye and greedily rubbed his hands together. Tim had only seen him do that when they had taken someone else's dessert. Tim was now certain that if there were anything in the forest, it would find them and it would kill them.

Julie dumbly nodded and crouched down even lower. Assuming Julie was taking his lead, Tim began to move stealthily through the underbrush, approaching the burned-out farmyard. Tim had never been one for stealth, and it seemed that with each step he took, a twig snapped or some sort of other bellowing announcement showed his presence to anything that could hear, see, or smell.

Looking behind him, Tim could not find Julie anywhere. He could not decide if this was a good thing or a bad one but decided to keep going.

As he reached the outskirts of the farm, he did not see anything amiss except for the burned-out husks of the house and outbuildings. Seeing the space in such disarray and silence brought a tinge of sadness to Tim's overly stressed heart. The Pumplekins had not been an exceptional lot of people, but he remembered many fun nights with several of their dimwitted daughters where either one, both, or himself were bent over a gate in the barn and were each too sore to sit down and enjoy a meal at the table after.

To his surprise, Tim heard something rustling in the barn, and with a sudden thrust of what he assumed was courage, he ran out into the short grass and announced himself to the barnyard.

"I ammmm Tim! Wizard of Halfass. Destroyer of pi... people! Who goes there?"

Tim was half certain his bumbling assistant had made his way into the barn and was in no way prepared for the hulking green creature that walked out of it. However, what he saw was not a goblin. Goblins were about the same size as halflings, just green and savage. This creature was a lot larger and much more muscular than any man Tim had seen in a long time. Tim sighed. This was a hobgoblin.

"What did you say, fat man? Something about pies?" the hobgoblin said, laughing wickedly.

Tim could see a grisly necklace of halfling ears and thumbs

around the beast's neck, and its green body was covered in the deep crimson of dried halfling blood.

"I… uh… I said people," stuttered Tim.

"Well, lucky for me then, porky. I am no man," the hobgoblin replied and spat as he slowly began to circle Tim.

The beast pulled out a wicked dagger from his deerskin cloth, and Tim could see the knife was soaked in the blood of his former friends. His predatory circling of Tim became tighter, like Tim circling the buffet for his second course.

"I am going to make you squeal louder than any of those half-bitches did, though I bet you won't be half as tasty," the beast exclaimed.

Tim seriously doubted that. With the gradual failing of his pancreas, Tim's blood became sweeter and sweeter each day. The hobgoblin licked his blade and began to walk directly towards Tim.

Tim had imagined this moment hundreds of times in his life: actual danger would approach, and he would die. However, instead of wetting himself, he found a sense of calm and shakily pulled out his short sword and channeled a bit of mana into his staff, which caused the gemstone contained within to glow. The hobgoblin must not have been expecting Tim to be an actual wizard, because with the channeling of his staff, the massive creature hissed and lunged at Tim.

Tim's temporary courage fled him immediately, and he tried to back away quickly. Instead, his legs became tangled, and he tumbled ungracefully to the ground.

The hobgoblin barked a laugh at him as he stood over Tim's trembling frame.

"This will not be quick," it said, showing off its wicked

fangs.

As it bent down to start its dastardly work, Tim's face was suddenly covered in a wash of hot blood. Tim screamed and as he desperately wiped the blood from his eyes, he saw the hobgoblin was frozen, his eyes distant, and one of the prongs of a pitchfork stuck out of his throat.

Tim crawled out from under the bloody dying beast and, to his surprise, saw Julie standing behind the fallen hobgoblin.

"Julie??" said Tim.

"Sneaky Julie," Julie said with almost no emotion behind his eyes.

"Julie?!" repeated Tim again, still in shock as his mind screamed at him that Julie was most likely a psychopath.

Julie sat down beside the hobgoblin and began to rifle through its pockets.

"Julie!" Tim screamed.

"You killed someone, and now you are looting his body. Where did you learn to do such things?"

Julie looked as though he didn't quite understand the question. Tim could see Julie skillfully separating the hobgoblin's loot into neat stacks and his devious little mind working.

"Julie grew up in capital, on streets. Sneak was life," said Julie casually.

Tim was dumbfounded. Besides pie, he had never heard Julie speak much about anything, and with his experience in Halfass, he assumed most halflings lived a blessed existence. Obviously, Julie had a very dark history behind him, and Tim was not sure if he wanted to know the whole of it.

Julie began to ramble on about a thieves guild, a child smuggling ring, and the like. But as often was his way, Tim decided to completely tune him out and focus on the task still at hand.

With the loot being properly separated, Tim decided he should at least look it over and see if it contained anything valuable.

There was a scattering of coins, a health potion, and a piece of paper. Tim looked over at Julie cleaning the thick blood off the wicked dagger, and with a flourish, it disappeared up his sleeve. Disturbed, Tim picked up the rest and opened up the piece of paper. To his surprise, it was a map of Halfass with various defensive structures marked.

"Was this hobgoblin planning to invade Halfass?" Tim said to himself

Either way, the plan for a campout was now over; he and Julie had to go back and discuss this with Sir Pog right away.

The walk back to town was a quiet one. Tim was too disturbed by the episode involving Julie to even eat anything, and as they reached the end of the forest, his stomach turned again. What had happened to Julie in the capital? Should Tim have listened to whatever rambling story the wee man had tried to share? His mind wandered back to the discovery of the hobgoblin. It had obviously been a brute; his clothing screamed of the outlands. Who could move a force undetected through the kingdoms?

As his mind wandered through all of the possibilities, his pace slowed as he began to smell a stench of sulfur in the air. Then, in the distance, he saw it. Halfass was on fire.

"KIIIIIIIIMMMMM!!" Tim wailed into the void like a tormented banshee.

Julie could not believe the speed at which his master's legs were moving; it was like watching a trotting pony with a broken leg. Well, not quite that fast, but impressive for Tim nonetheless. Julie trotted behind Tim, not yet breaking a sweat.

Julie stared in awe at the wealth of free meat and trinkets that lay strewn about the remnants of Halfass. He decided to take the opportunity to ease the suffering of some of the dead and dying by filling his pockets with some of the trinkets left behind.

Meanwhile, Tim continued his loud-breathing waddle up the main road of Halfass. He breathed heavily as he ran past the orphanage. Julie simply waved to the excited children. Tim dug deep as he ran by the hospital. Julie once again happily greeted the flaming individuals who were waving at him.

At last, Tim rounded the corner and saw his hole, Kim. She was a mess.

"Kim!!!!! Kim!!!! Kim!" Tim shrieked in a voice that was altogether not flattering to the ears of any man or beast.

Kim was a smoking ruin, a hole no man would dive in ever again. He dropped his things and attempted to run into Kim. Luckily, Julie had caught up and quickly tripped his master.

As Tim wallowed around on the earth, trying to rise up to reattempt his mad dash, Julie's hand suddenly covered his mouth. Tim noted absently that it did not smell of cheese, and then all he saw was black.

Tim's dreams were unsettled; again and again, he saw various calamities befalling his beloved hole, Kim.

The next morning, Tim awoke to the crackling sound and smells of cooking meat.

"Ahhhggh… Julie, I had the most unsettling dream," Tim said groggily, trying to pat away the thick white mat that lived on his tongue.

"Was it that Halfass was burned to the ground and Kim's hole was ruined beyond repair?" Julie said almost cheerily.

Tim winced.

"Yes, it was that exactly, Julie," responded the despondent wizard.

Julie looked down at the sausages he had collected and continued to go about his breakfast duties.

"Well, I hate to be the bearer of bad news, but I'm afraid

36

it wasn't a dream, master. I am truly sorry for your loss."

With his too-big eyes telling him it was true, though the strange, serene tone was confusing, Tim tried desperately not to take in his surroundings, but it was to no avail.

Everywhere Tim turned, he saw destruction.

The brewers had been brewed, the bakers baked, and what had happened to many others… well, he hadn't the heart to describe. As he stood, he considered going into Kim's hole one last time, but before he could, Julie offered him some breakfast.

"Uncut sausage, sir?" the grinning little monster asked.

"Uncut?" Tim asked disgustedly.

"Yes, for some odd reason these sausages I found scattered around Halfass all seem to have hoods on the end of them. Some of them were even still attached at the root…" Julie replied.

Tim began to wonder where and what Julie thought sausages were, but before he could, they both turned as a trumpet tooted in the distance. Tim simply did not have the motivation to go and see who was trumpeting this early in the morning, so instead, he sent Julie to see who was making all the racket. Begrudgingly leaving his prepared sausages, Julie marched out of town and left his master to his grief.

Julie had never seen Tim so distraught, and he honestly had no idea how he was going to pull him out of this one. As he pondered, Julie found that with all its citizens murdered, he could make excellent time getting to the edge of the village. In around three minutes, he approached the outskirts and saw an assembled mass of men and beasts in the distance. However, they were not green, so he assumed they were not mean.

Approaching the host, Julie stopped in the middle of the burned field and asked,

"Who goes there? In the name of Tim, the wizard of Halfass!" sounding reasonably convincing for a man heralding in a smoking ruin.

A tall man with an excellent beard and shiny armor approached Julie and said,

"I go there, along with my army. I am Sir Eric Von Shinerbock, Lord Protector of the Western Shield and High Captain of the Queen's Green Guard. Your master is the wizard of Halfass? This, Tim?"

Julie nodded dumbly.

Sir Eric noted a bit of spittle running down the mutated halfling's cheek and didn't know if he was slow or perhaps had survived the attack with some sort of brain injury. Touching the little man, Eric instantly regretted it, finding the creature's entire body seemed to be sweaty even though the morning was quite cool. He quickly pulled his hand away, though unable to avoid the viscous substance that was left on his fingers.

"Great… Why don't you go over to the healer's tent… lad?" the knight asked, never taking his eyes off the little man or removing his hand from his ever-ready sword.

Julie nodded once again and proceeded to head in the wrong direction. Eric very reluctantly touched Julie once again and pointed him in the right direction, adding,

"Once you're all checked out, we will go and see this master of yours."

Tim is quite a stupid name for a wizard, Eric thought to himself, but little did he know what other trouble Tim would cause for him yet. Once Julie had been thoroughly checked by several healers and, to Eric's surprise, had been told he suffered no injuries, he sent the little monster off to collect Tim with a scroll bearing his mark.

After a bit of a wrestle and the promise of more sausages, Tim reluctantly agreed to return with Julie and meet with Sir Eric. As Tim approached the commander's tent, sweat and anxiety swept over him. As the town wizard of one of the western shield states, Tim was technically under the command of Sir Eric. However, since Halfass was too far for anyone to really visit and Tim never wanted to leave, the two of them meeting had always been unlikely. Now the first time they would meet was under the circumstances of Tim's charge being totally destroyed, and Tim would be marked as suspiciously absent during the attack.

Tim thought of these things and more, but the worn-out devastation of his hole, Kim, kept playing over and over in his mind.

His great book of recipes hadn't even been spared; countless tastes lost to the void. Why should he even go on? As he entered the tent, feeling what he imagined was the lowest level of morose, Tim found that he could fall even further. The impressive group of individuals that sat before him would have gone perfectly in one of his many adventure books, which also were now nothing but a pile of ash.

Sir Eric sat resplendent in his glittering plate and mail. As Tim entered, the knight stood, and Tim could see a trace amount of red emanating from his large bastard sword. The rest of the party looked equally impressive: two guards in gold plate armor etched in green, a dwarf that looked like he could take on a mountain, and a gigantic she-beast in thin leather, wielding a wicked-looking two-handed axe. As Tim took in the large weapon, the tent flaps parted, and in stepped the most beautiful woman he had ever seen. She was clad in all white, with a matching staff, and even her hair was so blonde that it could have matched her robes. To his own shame, his eyes immediately fell on her impressive bosom, and as far as Tim could tell, all of her skin was ivory.

As Tim stared slack-jawed, the young mage became concerned.

"Sir Eric, is this another invalid you wish to have tested? I can tell straight away something is wrong with this one," Aurora asked with real concern in her voice.

"No, no, my dear. I believe he is just taking in the sights," replied Sir Eric with a chuckle.

"I... I... uh... I... Tim," Tim stammered.

"Are you sure?" Aurora asked, even more worry growing in her voice.

She continued to look at Sir Eric but did not get the joke. Eric slapped Tim across the back of the shoulder. The blow was enough to stagger Tim, and honestly, it hurt quite a bit. However, since there was a lady present, Tim bravely held back his tears.

"Yes Aurora, he's... mostly fine," Eric said, not sounding entirely convinced himself.

"He is actually one of your own, a wizard... This is Tim, the former town wizard of Halfass."

Tim nodded dumbly, and sadly noted the use of the word former.

"Oh, you poor dear," Aurora cooed.

Noticing that she did not sound at all disgusted with him yet, Tim remembered that the sympathy route often paid dividends...

"Yes, I am very upset," Tim said while making a sort of cringey sad face.

This seemed to scare Aurora, and as she took Tim's hand, she immediately regretted it. His fingers were greasy, and his whole body smelled of strange and forbidden meats.

"My… my apologies. I had several half-hooded sausages this morning and didn't have time to clean up."

Aurora simply nodded, with a clear look of disgust on her face. She then turned and said,

"Sir Eric, we have a note from moth… ahem… from the capital. They seem to have a lead on what has caused all of this."

Eric took the paper, and Tim decided that since he had now done his duty, maybe it was a good time to slink off back to town and wallow for a few days. Maybe he could cash in this Aurora chip some other time when they had less going on.

Tim stood to leave.

"Wait, Tim, it seems this might be of some interest to you; this says something about a witch, a former classmate of yours?" Eric handed him the parchment.

Tim hadn't thought of any of his classmates in an age; most of them had died heroically in some place or another. So, he was surprised to hear that one still lived. As he read over the paper, the name immediately jumped out at him: Eliza Slagbottom.

"Slagbottom?" he mumbled to himself.

He remembered the girl, a piggish thing that was almost as dirty as him in school; she had a dumpy look to her, and not even the animals had found her attractive. As Tim remembered, they both had been fighting to not be at the bottom of the class. She came in dead last, and instead of receiving the comfy job as wizard of Halfass, she was politely banished to a human settlement on the border of the outlands.

"As I remember, Eliza and the rest of her town were murdered sixty years ago by raiders, carried off to the wilds and never to be seen again," Tim said confidently, proud that he remembered something useful.

"That's right," Eric replied, "but it appears it didn't take. The girl has taken to the dark arts and now leads quite the host of green ones."

"Aye, we've known of such things to happen even amongst our kind," grumbled the menacing dwarf, speaking for the first time.

"Oh yes, how rude of me. Tim, this is Ayers Gravelrock, ambassador of the western dwarven clans and famous hammer-man."

Tim made a sort of awkward wave.

"And this is Leslie," Eric said, pointing to the large barbarian woman who was currently picking her teeth with a bone.

"Leslie? A bit odd for a barbarian, isn't it?" Tim said with a laugh.

"Really?" Leslie said sarcastically. "A fat wizard with dick-greased fingers wants to give me grief over MY name?"

"I didn't mean..." Tim stammered.

"Aye, that's what I thought, wee man," Leslie grunted and adjusted something rather large in the front of her skirt. Tim pondered for a moment why she had said the phrase dick-greased but decided to shrug it off.

Eric side-stepped this exchange and continued,

"...And you have already met one of our healers, Aurora.

Freshly graduated from the Myrmidon Wizards College and first in her class."

Aurora curtsied to Tim.

"Quite a party you lot have; I wish you the best of luck. I am afraid I have much to do; my hole was destroyed by a host of ravenous goblinoids, and I'm afraid I can't even sit down at the moment…" Tim said as he turned towards the exit.

"Tim," Sir Eric cut in. "You are the only living mage that knows Eliza. This group is set to head off and follow a lead about her. If she's there, your personal relationship could prove to be invaluable to the cause."

Tim's face went white.

"M… me?" whined Tim.

"Yes Tim, you are a trained wizard, are you not?" Sir Eric asked.

"Well, yes of course, Sir Eric, but it's been… well I… I hardly even know Eliza! I doubt she would remember me…" Tim lied. "And if I am being totally honest, I have never actually gone on a quest…"

"What? But Tim, all wizards must pass a trial before accepting a post?" Aurora asked curiously.

"Well…" Tim started and immediately looked down at the floor. "I… I had a note for that day, and since I was already accepted by Halfass, they felt I didn't actually need to pass a trial. The odds of me facing anything were so slim, and word of my other abilities had already reached them…"

The entire group stared at Tim blankly. They did not know what to say.

After the lull reached an embarrassingly long time, Ayers broke the silence:

"Well, Sir Eric, given I have gone on such expeditions countless times myself, I don't mind leading this group of misfits."

"I also will throw in my axe. I would love to see this little piggy…" Leslie paused, "…in action."

"Oh, how wonderful! I would like to also come along; the party needs a proper healer after all. I am also happy to prepare a salve for your hole if you so desire, Tim," Aurora said and was the only person in the tent that didn't have to hide a smile.

Eric gave a hesitant glance at Aurora when she made this statement but said nothing. The group seemed satisfied with itself, and Tim decided if he was going to have to participate, he knew just the halfling to round out the group.

"Well, since everyone is so dead set on this, I suppose I also know a rogue," Tim said happily, thinking of the misery it would bring Julie.

*T*im was moving even more slowly than usual as he dragged his feet through the dirt and ash back to his ruined hole, Kim. Tim wasn't sure what Aurora's salve was supposed to help; so far, all it had done was make his tongue numb.

When he thought of what Julie would say about being recruited for an adventure, he could almost summon the ghost of a smile. As he walked, he thought of how lovely a nap in his sleep chair would be right now. But alas, it was gone, and so too was his nap chair, nap couch, comfy reading nook, and the host of bedrooms that he slept in for various reasons. They were all gone. His sacred herb had been burned in a way that no one could enjoy. All of his stashes of various treats melted and cooked beyond recovery. He had spent part of the morning trying to scrape the carbonized remains of some honey from a pot but just wound up getting it stuck on his hand like an idiot.

As he arrived at the ruined opening that used to be Kim's hole, he saw to his true dismay that Julie seemed to be actually enjoying himself. The little miscreant was stacking parts of bodies like cordwood and had even made a little fort. Julie was happily marching literal finger puppets up the little door when he saw Tim approach. Once again Tim decided that questions would lead to answers that he did not want to hear, so he decided not to address this at all. Tim instead coughed to interrupt the disturbing scene.

"Julie, we have been selected for a most important job. You and I will be joining a group of adventurers and heading off to find the person or beast responsible for all of this," Tim said, waving his arm to indicate the general devastation around them.

"Me? What will I be doing on an adventure Tim?" Julie replied in a shocked tone.

"Well, Julie, as your future therapist will most likely tell you, you are far more than meets the eye. And after that impressive display of sneaking back at the Pumplekins' farm," —Tim said the word sneaking while making finger parentheses—"I decided to nominate you as the official... err sneaker of the group."

"Sneaker..." Julie replied, with a dead, doll-like stare encompassing his excessively large black eyes. After a flurry of conflicting emotions as well as an external discussion with himself, Julie excitedly exclaimed,

"I accept, master! I will be the best sneaker ever; Julie will be quiet and move like the wind or air... Yes, Air Julie!"

Tim just rolled his eyes and patted his considerable paunch. He wondered if Julie had any more sausages lying around.

After a bit of a snack, the two continued to pick through the remains of Kim's hole. Like any good hole she had secret depths that only the most dedicated of delvers could discover. To that effect Tim and Julie stumbled across a small cache of desserts one of them had hidden at one point or another from the other.

As the sun set, the pair ate the last of their Halfass treats and headed for the camp.

*T*he night before the outing beset Tim with a tornado of digestional pain, the likes of which he had rarely experienced in his many years of intense eating. At one point, several of the guards lined the outside of the latrine and made disparaging comments that did not help with Tim's general anxiety.

With Tim's food properly poisoned, Julie knew he had several hours to himself and made his way back to his secret haunt. With practiced hands and speed like that of a chronic masturbator, Julie quickly dove into the pile of rubble that concealed his own hole. He had appropriately called it Tim and, to his dismay, found it equally as ruined as Kim. The monsters appeared to have thoroughly destroyed Julie's altars, bone puppets, and secret meat locker. He even found where they had stolen the decoy recipe book.

"Foolish corporeals," Julie muttered under his breath.

He never understood why these temporary beings went through so much trouble, but that was a philosophical discussion for another time. Julie picked up a few of his favorite travel-sized bones and stuck them in his pouch along with the actual recipe book. Then, upon the bones of his favorite miniature skull, he swore that they would all pay — when it was convenient and did not cause him too much trouble of course. With that, Julie plodded off to check on Tim's projectile situation.

8

With the rising sun, Tim found his bowels and nerves had settled, and the real work was about to begin. The group set off on what must have been the farthest distance that Tim had ever walked in his whole life. As they marched, Tim began to grow angry with the incessant exercise. He was tired and hungry, his ass hurt, and he had already eaten all the numbing salve gifted to him by Aurora. The rest of the group seemed to be built for the wilds. All of them were covered in lean muscle, and each had a set of tools honed for their trade. Even the smallest of the group, Aurora, was carrying a pack much larger than Tim.

After just an hour of walking, Tim and Julie found themselves falling behind while the rest of the group powered on. Then after a short while longer, Tim and Julie lost sight of the group altogether, and they were forced to rely on Julie's tracking ability.

"Are you sure we are going the right way?" Tim asked as he desperately sucked in air.

"I smell something."

This had been Julie's response every other time Tim had asked as well. As Tim finally accepted that he and Julie would most likely die of exposure in the wilderness, with one or the other finally falling prey to some sort of cannibalistic showdown, the sound of laughter began to trickle down from the next clearing.

"Sweet Pies!!" Tim bellowed.

It was their camp.

Tim and Julie trundled into the clearing to find the rest of their party sitting around an unlit campfire, drinking and taking their ease. He noticed that the camp was already in shipshape condition, with each tent a proper home away from home for its occupant.

He also noticed that Leslie's tent was especially tall, and as he looked back to the tent Julie was trying to erect, he felt more than a little pole envy.

Walking up to the group, Tim promptly lay on the ground and began to wring out all the moisture he could from his swampy bulk.

"I guess walking wasn't something a wizard did much in Halfass?" Leslie said snarkily, motioning to Tim's quaking bulk.

Between gasps, Tim let out,

"Well, to be the wizard of a place like Halfass, it really helps to immerse yourself in the local culture."

The group laughed.

"So, tell us then lad. What exactly is the culture of the half-ones? As I understand, the little lechers mostly just breed, eat, and sleep," Ayers said.

"That is it entirely," Tim said wistfully, finally catching his breath.

The group answered this with another round of laughter. Tim didn't find the humor in what he considered a perfect lifestyle.

"If you don't mind me asking, Tim, what exactly did your usual duties require?" said Aurora. "Before I left the college, I considered taking a town position, but I found most of them to be a bit boring."

"Well..." Tim started trying to think of something to say, then Leslie interrupted.

"Before Tim entertains us with tales of his slovenly glory, why doesn't the little magey boy give us a demonstration? To be honest, I am not entirely sure IF he's even a wizard at all. Maybe just a big dumb lad who stumbled on a cushy job. Go on then... light the fire for us... wizard."

This was surprising, thought Tim. No one had actually asked him to do any sort of magic, well, since... he couldn't really remember the last time. The encounter with the hobgoblin at the Pumplekins' farm had made him infuse his staff with power, but he didn't actually end up doing anything. Standing up off the ground, he announced,

"That's... that's absurd Leslie! That would be like me asking you to prove that you are, in fact, a woman. A fact that I am still on the fence about, I'll have you know. So, I don't think, I don't think..."

"It's fine, Tim. Just a spout of fire will shut her up good," Ayers said, slapping Tim on the back, but the set of his eyes was serious. Tim nervously looked back at Ayers and begrudgingly began to lift his staff and focus.

Nothing happened.

Tim focused again, and as he became even more nervous, his mind began to instinctively think about the emotional turmoil cookies that he would have Julie make any time he was feeling nervous or scared. They were the most perfect mixture of chocolate, oatmeal, marshmallow, and other various delicacies. Then, as his mouth began to drool over the thought of cookies, he was overwhelmed with a sudden rush of relief and surprise.

He had found it. With the application of his will, the very matter that bound the universe together was his to command. He could feel it flow from everything to everywhere, and with the mumble of some arcane words that he managed to bring forth from the deep recesses of his memory, he conjured fire into existence.

A small, pitiful, limp gout of flame sprayed itself onto the eagerly waiting wood pile.

It wasn't an impressive stream, and the fact that the gout of flame had gone limp halfway through the exercise certainly did not impress anyone. But he had done it.

"Fire! I have made fire!" Tim shrieked to the heavens while banging on his chest. Julie seemed most impressed as he casually stroked his cheek.

"See?" Tim said, boastfully.

The rest of the group nodded. He had technically made fire.

"Hmmmph," Leslie snorted. "I hope you can wield your other wand better than that."

After Tim's most impressive showing of fire magic, the group began chattering about this and that as they prepared for the evening meal. Julie, it seemed, had stolen a rather large portion of ham from the captain's tent, much to the delight of the entire party.

As they ate their meal and drank some strong dwarven ale, the group all shared a bit about themselves… and Tim was finally able to have a bit of a sit. About an hour passed, and after Ayers had regaled the group with tales of his incredible history, Leslie had begun and was just finally finishing her, err… tale of conquest.

"So, you see, it wasn't technically taboo. Turns out Kobolds don't have specific mating rules regarding cannibalism!" Leslie said, beaming with pride.

The rest of the group sat in stunned silence at the finish of her tale. Tim was expecting a brief background on each of them, not a torrid story of sexual discovery and conquest amongst the dog men of the underground. Trying to erase his memory of the event, he turned to Aurora.

"Aurora, I don't suppose you have a much tamer story to tell?" Tim asked, not ever wanting to look over at Leslie again.

Aurora nodded and made a slight glance down at Tim's shirt. To his non-surprise, there was a large spattering of grease on it. To his actual surprise, he felt a bit of shame.

Shame?! How long had it been since he had felt that? During his dozens of years of feasting and rolling around with Julie, they had lived in what Tim had felt was a natural state: men of the wild. Now he began to wonder if he had the wrong idea the entire time. Keeping perfectly proper, Aurora stood and addressed the group.

"I know with Tim asking about me, you all probably have questions. This, after all, is my first assignment out of school, and I would like to tell you all a bit about me and who I am."

The group nodded. Why not? The woods were awfully boring.

"I was born Aurora Flamegash," she started.

Tim's immediate instinct was to make a clear and obvious joke about drapes, but he somehow kept it down, though he thought something inside him might die. He realized he was focusing too much on his inner dialogue and started listening to Aurora again.

"…my parents, Mr. and Mrs. Flamegash…"

Dammit, Tim. No.

"…are the industrious merchants of the seaside town of Myrmidon. Growing up, I lived a privileged life. Servants waiting on me hand and foot. My older brother embraced this life, and I am ashamed to say, will never be much of anything, living a life of leisure and excess."

Tim lost his focus here once again; it sounded like that bastard had it even better than him! Just imagine what all he could do with an infinite supply of coin and no responsibilities. That had always been his actual dream. While Tim's Halfass setup would've been the envy of most, the fear of actually having to work had always held him back. As Aurora rambled on about her story, Tim now looked at her in a new light. He thought, no, he knew, he loved her.

"…and after putting out the flames and reviving that desperate child, I knew I wanted to make a mark on this world."

Tim looked around, and the others were all in tears, but not Tim; he was grinning from ear to ear.

"Can you hear the thunder?" muttered Julie.

"What are you on about, Julie? There isn't a cloud in the sky," Tim said, once again pushing Julie's thoughts out of his mind.

The party had broken camp with the rising of the sun after being treated to sausages by Julie.

But this was no sausage party.

"So, Aurora… I must say, your salve worked wonders for me last night. My tongue hasn't felt this moist in ages!"

Aurora, confused, gave Tim a sideways glance and moved hastily towards Leslie. The group was walking quickly towards the rising sun, and it occurred to Tim that he wasn't sure where they were going. Tim slowed his pace to walk beside Julie. He knew he could get his dimwitted companion to ask.

"Julie, ask Ayers where we're going," Tim whispered to the furry halfling creature.

Julie was idly picking his ear and then shrugged with indifference.

"Beard man," Julie announced cavalierly.

"Yes, master Julie?" Ayers responded.

"Where are we going, sir? I know it's to find the baddie. But no one has said where she is?"

"Very astute of you, Julie. I appreciate a man… well, a half-man, who wants to know where he is going."

Julie beamed at this, and Aurora turned and patted him on the head. Tim couldn't believe this. He had skipped breakfast, washed himself, and was exercising early in the morning, and Julie, with the personality and hygiene of a filled chamber pot, was getting praised for asking his question?

"It was actually my idea for him to ask," Tim said, putting on a prideful air.

"What a coward," Leslie replied as she licked her meat-stained fingers.

"Coward? You want to bark that nonsense with half-sausage on your breath?" Tim said, deflating a bit.

"Half-sausage?" Aurora mouthed quietly.

"Enough all o' you!" Ayers said. "We haven't the time for squabbling, and we will be getting close soon anyway. Whoever wanted to know, we are going to an old dwarven outpost."

"An outpost out here?" Aurora asked, surprised. "I wasn't aware there were any dwarven settlements this close to the kingdoms."

"There isn't," Ayers replied.

"Then why—" Aurora started.

"We used to have interests out here. You forget you menfolk are relatively new for the older races of the world. Dwarves, Elves, Greens, and some of the other folk have lived in this world far longer, and our histories ebb and flow like the tide. This wood is nothing now but a half-forgotten forest in a halfling kingdom that is nothing more than a buffer state for the realms of men. An age ago or more now, I canny' remember, this forest stretched for a week's ride or more in all directions. A great kingdom of elves dwelled here, and they grew the forest like a halfling grows a melon. Trees the likes I'd never seen before or since. Was enough that even my people would come up from the ground to walk amongst it. The capital, or what served for one, was about a day's walk from here. We raised our tunnel far enough from it not to disturb some of the great trees. That tunnel had been filled in, and its access to the great Down Under was sealed."

"Tree melons?" Julie exclaimed, excitedly.

"If it was sealed, then why do we need to go check it?" Tim said, actually paying attention to Ayer's story.

"Hmm… err, beardy man, you said tree melons? Please tell me more," Julie checked again.

"What is that one on about?" Ayers asked curiously, nodding towards Julie. He continued, "Just because it was closed, doesn't mean it can't be reopened. There are tunnels that even we have forgotten. But if the green ones are this far inside the kingdom, an underground route makes the most sense, and this is the only one that's close enough to work."

The only noticeable difference as they began to approach the outpost was the thinning of the trees. The entire walk from the camp, the group had been surrounded by royal oak giants as tall as any Tim had ever seen. However, an hour later, the trees were still massive but noticeably smaller than some of the others.

"We're getting close now. We had to harvest the timber around here to build the supports for the original tunnel. Of course, we replaced it with stone like most of the Under, but nothing beats timber on the first go-round. It was hard even for us. The trees were so beautiful," Ayers said remorsefully.

Soon, Leslie guided the group to an overgrown stone walkway. Though, it hadn't been used in hundreds of years, the dwarven stone was still strong and true.

"Feels good to have dwarven stone under my feet," Ayers crowed. "Can't believe it might have been violated by those green bastards!"

The stone path led them to a large, forested hill and then straight into the earth from there. Tim found the entrance to be remarkable, a polished stone entryway with some of the finest stonework he had ever seen.

"Was this the capital of the Dwarves?" Tim asked.

Ayers laughed, and exclaimed,

"Merely a pit stop, lad. The stonework of the great under cities would leave you breathless for days!"

The cavern's opening had been fashioned into the shape of a large dwarven head, complete with a beard and their stylized battle helmet. The road led directly into its mouth. Before the group entered, Leslie picked something up off the ground, sniffed it, and then ate a small piece.

"Goblin shit," Leslie said, with a subtle excitement in her

voice as she swallowed the morsel.

This gave even Julie pause. Each member of the party took out a small torch and lit it, then gathered around the entryway.

"Leslie and I will go first and scout out the two main paths. Both halls lead down to the underkeep," said Ayers.

Tim thought this sounded like an excellent idea. Dwarves could see in pitch blackness, and he imagined if Leslie couldn't see, she could probably sniff out anything around her. The only one that seemed to be put off by this plan was Aurora.

"And what am I supposed to do?" Aurora's eyes clearly indicated towards Tim and Julie.

Ayers nodded with a look that was very sympathetic but said,

"You all will serve as backup. We will need healing and gods know what else after messing around in this horrid hole."

Aurora sighed and nodded. Tim and Julie were oblivious to the exchange since they both had the social maturity of six-year-olds raised by feral cats. All Tim heard was that he was not facing any imminent danger and could stay up here and stare at Aurora. Although, admittedly, it had been a while since he had wooed a woman. For the halfling women, the promise of a full carrot instead of a half had been enough, but Aurora was differ-ent. She made Tim's carrot... nervous. He did not want another repeat of the staff incident. Sure, getting to the climax is great and all, but a little show can really boost the old self-esteem.

At this point, Aurora began to wave at Tim to try and draw away some of the awkwardness. Ayers and Leslie had been gone for five minutes, and Tim had just been staring at her slack-jawed, with the smallest of noticeable bumps under his too-thin robe. He also kept strangely mentioning how much he enjoyed her salve.

This made her more and more uncomfortable.

"Well, no reason for us to just stand about. Why don't we have a bit of a stroll and see if there's anything useful lying around," Aurora said in an attempt to escape the situation.

Tim and Julie sighed as one… moving… again.

Leslie could smell things — many horrid, unwashed things all around her. She wanted to just follow her nose, but that would likely lead her down to the goblin's latrine. She had to focus her powers and stay on the task at hand. She removed her shoes and could feel a thick layer of mossy filth covering the old flagstones. This made her as quiet as a cat, and as she continued to descend, she could hear a growing chorus of small, strangled voices.

Rounding a corner at the end of the last stairwell, she found herself at a door overlooking a huge open cavern. It was most likely a natural cave that had been hollowed out and expanded by the Dwarves.

"Enterprising little fuckers," Leslie muttered to herself.

Leslie didn't care for Dwarves much, but even she could admit they were masters at shaping stone. Before her, an old dwarven fortress stood in the middle of a great expanse. Two stone roads led out of it. The closest road had been destroyed at some point, and the fine dwarven stonework yawned off into the great black oblivion below. Where the road had been destroyed, however, a patchwork of crudely worked wooden scaffolding connected the structure to its other end in the distance.

"So, that's how those little green shits got in..."

The goblins had cobbled together a workaround and now had access to the soft underbelly of the civilized realms. There was a part of her that didn't mind at all. Imagine the chaos that would reign if a green horde appeared out of nowhere and began to ravage all the safe places. That would be the time for a barbarian to shine. However, another part of her mind knew how terrible that would be. Most of the world was already like that, a brutal place ruled by brutal beings who try to snuff out anything beautiful; she knew it all too well.

Her remembrance stopped short when she saw a column of particularly brutal-looking goblins marching several levels below her. They were led by a couple of great brutal hobs, each dragging one leg of a very bloody, and very angry, Ayers.

Meanwhile, back at the entrance, Tim nudged Julie suggestively. Julie coughed rather loudly at Aurora and spat out,

"Wouldn't it be funny if we played like dare or pickle or something?!"

"Dare or pickle? Aurora replied shyly and slightly disgustedly. "Julie, what is that game?"

Julie giggling,

"Oh, you've never played? We always used to play it in the slave pits. You either dare someone, or you put your—"

"That's quite enough, Julie. Please don't show me," Aurora interrupted and patted Julie's hand as he was rapidly trying to undo his britches.

He then looked directly at Tim and made an over-exaggerated

wink. Tim could only groan; he had told Julie to be smooth. That was… well… he should've actually been thankful it wasn't worse. Tim tried not to look too bashful as he stood in the dirty corner and idly kicked an old dwarven skull, looking like an obese, sweaty wildebeest trying to act coy. As he and Julie moved closer, Aurora began to have the look of a hunted animal with nowhere to run. Once Leslie's lumbering frame appeared from around a corner, Aurora nearly jumped her bones.

"Les! Thank God you're here!! We were so worried, right guys?" Aurora said, relief clearly evident on her face.

Tim actually took note of this and assumed Aurora had been getting annoyed with Julie again — not that he blamed her. They all changed their tune, however, when Leslie explained what was going on. Tim tried not to be too upset and would prepare his pickle for another day.

"Ayers is tied up and will be tortured and killed, so we don't have time to nap or play or whatever in the gods' names you people do. We have to act hard and fast."

The dare or pickle trio all nodded.

"Well…" Leslie said in an anticipating tone.

"Well, what? You're the only one who has been down there. You know what we are facing and how to get there. You have to lead Leslie," Tim said in a rare moment of coherent thought. This seemed to make Leslie nervous, but she simply nodded and stood up.

"Fine… follow me, magic people."

"Magic people," Tim said disgustedly. "We aren't vagrants, dammit; we are wizards! Well, Julie is a vagrant."

The foursome made their way to Leslie's previous vantage point and took stock of the scene below. Ayers was in a tight spot, a very tight spot. From their vantage, it looked as though he had already been beaten and stripped of most of his armor.

"Damn, he's in a tight spot," said Tim.

"A very tight spot," Leslie echoed.

"Do they want to know about the tree melons as well?" questioned Julie, still oblivious to the danger that awaits.

Tight spots naturally made Tim think of Aurora, so he looked over at her long enough for her to get uncomfortable and change positions. Tim thought about how things seemed to be going quite well as he strummed his fingers against his flabby cheeks.

"Tim, stop petting yourself and get over here," Leslie sneered.

"I wasn't... I'm not—" Tim was shushed by both of the females. "But you just—"

"Shh!" Leslie reiterated.

Tim very stealthily stood up and nearly fell off from the high platform. Falling to his knees, he shuffled himself over by Leslie, knocking down a loose brick into the ether.

"We have a plan," Aurora said.

As she told Tim the plan, his face got paler and paler.

"**I**'m really in it now…" Tim thought as he continued his stealth knee shuffle just under the lip of the stone wall that ringed the dwarven roadway.

He just kept reminding himself what was all riding on this. Also, he was surprised that his single command to Julie was so far being followed.

"Sneak," the little monster repeated somewhere behind Tim.

All he had to do was survive this whole endeavor, hope that the kingdoms weren't destroyed in the process, woo Aurora, and then live in the lap of her parents' wealth for the rest of his days. That life would make his old hole, Kim, look like a one-potato girl in a two-potato world.

Tim began to imagine all the delicacies available to someone like that. My gods, the pies.

This was dangerous territory for him to think about at the moment. He had a job to do, and he was almost sure he could do it. Speaking of which, Tim began to waddle his knees even faster, and at last, he reached the wooden scaffolding.

Aurora and Leslie crept silently down the winding stairs. As the two reached the bottom, they gave Tim a reassuring wave and slipped off down a side passage. Idly, Aurora wondered how safe it was to have discount wizarding schools like the one Tim must have attended. Was it safe? Was it legal to barely train people like that and allow them to call themselves wizards? Much less to be hardly adequate in the most basic abilities and then to be given a posting nonetheless, even if it was for a small village of mutants. It was mind-boggling.

Her thoughts faded to the back of her mind when Leslie lifted a shit-stained finger to Aurora's lips.

"In no way was that needed or necessary," Aurora said with an authoritative snap.

She would address that at a later date. Leslie removed her finger and motioned towards a short half-stairwell leading to a sublevel right above them. She then removed a wicked-looking dagger from somewhere on her person and crept through the door first. Aurora followed, and as they entered, Leslie struck like a snake on a half-asleep guard, nearly decapitating the creature with her crude blade. Black blood exploded from the beast and pooled all around his now limp body. Leslie was smiling wickedly.

"Never gets old. It really doesn't," she whispered to herself.

Aurora now wished she was with Tim, and even Julie with his pickle.

Tim wished he was anywhere else in the world at that moment, but instead, he was shuffling across a goblin bridge that hung over a never-ending precipice with a now humming Julie in tow.

On one end of this bridge was an ancient dwarven keep overrun by goblins that were torturing a member of his party, and on the other end… well… the gods knew what was over there. Somehow, through all of this, Tim was putting himself directly in the middle of it.

Tim made his way a decent distance from the start of the bridge and looked back towards the keep. Aurora was going to create a small flash in a window above the courtyard as his signal to create the diversion. Tim wanted the signal to come so that he knew she was alright, but he also didn't want it to come so he wouldn't have to do anything. Just as he thought this, a small white light flashed in a faraway window, like a candle being blown in the wind, and he knew that was it.

"Here we fucking go…" mumbled Tim, condescendingly.

The plan was for Tim to do his little flamethrower stunt off the side of the bridge. The fire should be bright enough to get their attention and take some of the goblins off of Ayers. That would make a window for the other two to pounce down and take the rest of them out. Once Ayers was freed, the three would come to Tim's rescue in turn.

To be honest, Tim didn't think it all quite made sense, but in his heart, he knew Aurora would never hurt him. He believed they were to be married after all.

Standing up, Tim readied himself and began to say the arcane words of power. For some reason, whenever Tim was going to use magic, his mind often drifted to his trusty recipe book.

"Mmm, fire…"

This made him think of page sixty-three, toasted oatmeal cookies. You needed to add just the right amount of cinnamon for a tasty surprise. Realizing he was getting sidetracked, he found himself mouthing the words of his recipe,

"Eggs, oatmeal, milk…."

As the words of the recipe left his lips, this time instead of a pathetic premature burst, his staff unexpectedly shot forth a hardy thick stream from its tip. A gout of flame shot forth into the black and burned hot and bright enough that it looked in the dark as if a strand of the sun had been brought down into the cave.

Leslie and Aurora were both stunned by the display below them. In fact, if they had not been looking away while coming up with a backup plan at the time, the two very well might have been blinded by Tim's spray.

As Leslie looked below, she saw most of the goblins lying on the ground around Ayers, wallowing in pain from being blinded by the light. She could also see Julie wallowing around at Tim's feet shrieking in pain. He had obviously looked directly at the light.

This was it; she leapt to the ground below, pulling yet another concealed dagger from her person, and began her deadly work. In an open battle, nothing made the gender-fluid, shit-eating barbarian happier than letting her axe sing its destructive song. In close quarters, however, her daggers were much more useful. She used one hob to break her fall, and before his bones were done crunching under her boots, she had felled the other with a swipe of her blades. The five or six stunned and blinded goblins quickly fell beneath her, and by the time Aurora arrived, they were all dead and she was unshackling Ayers from his bonds.

"About time, ladies," the gruff dwarf said as the last of his chains fell away, "and where are the others?"

"Tim is off creating a distraction. He's the one that blinded them!" Aurora said in disbelief. "But it seems to have blinded Julie as well…”

Ayers looked impressed and not surprised.

“Maybe more to that one than just that unkempt bulk!”

Aurora nodded; maybe there was.

The trio quickly took off down the stone bridge to meet the remaining goblins and save Tim and Julie. Tim was definitely in need of saving. As his flames died out, four or five goblins began stumbling out of the darkness towards him, no doubt attracted by Julie’s wailing cries.

He didn’t know if it was an inherent goblin trait, but as soon as they could see again, they all began making pig sounds at him, just like the hob from Halfass. Tim readied himself for another spell and was about to begin reciting the recipe for a warm, buttered blueberry muffin when he heard something behind him.

Turning, Tim saw another goblin patrol emerging out of the black, and at its head stood none other than Eliza Slagbottom.

The lizard part of Tim’s brain immediately processed the danger at hand with the veritable army of monsters behind her, but the smallest head of Tim noticed the startling changes to Eliza’s physique.

“Well, well, if it isn’t the former master of Kim’s hole. Last I saw of her, she looked more stretched out than your waistline, Timothy.”

Tim did not even notice the stinging remark about his home or body.

“Eliza? You… you…” Tim stuttered.

“Yes, I am quite attractive now. Perhaps you shouldn’t have been so dismissive of me in school, Tim. The dark one knows the fun we could have had. Now I wouldn't let you share a bed with my dog."

"I wasn't ever mean to you Eliza," Tim said, searching his memories.

"What!?" the witch shrieked, and her eyes turned a dark shade of purple. "You were my tormentor! ...Slag Bottom, Hag Bottom. Eliza is so ugly a dog wouldn't lick her with a bewitchment?!"

Purple fire enveloped her hands. Tim's mind began to have a dim memory of one or two of those... incidents.

"I uh... I hmmm," Tim said without any confidence.

"I wish you were worth the effort of my anger, Tim. I killed the halflings because of you. I wanted you to hurt first, I am only sorry that you missed the party. No matter, you are here now. Though before I kill you, there is something I want you to know."

At this, Eliza approached Tim and vindictively whispered into his ear,

"I destroyed your recipes."

"No!" Tim screamed.

At that moment of impetus, the goblins began to charge him, and as Eliza walked away, she turned back to Tim.

"I took away your Kim because of what you took from me. Now, I will take it from everyone else!"

She then began to cast. However, her cast was cut short when, out of nowhere, Julie appeared and jumped onto Eliza like a crazed boxer, going directly for her ear, all the while screaming,

"You broke my bone friends!"

With a shriek, she cast the husky halfling back at Tim and finished her spell. As soon as the arcane words left her mouth, purple flames leapt up and covered the small bridge in broiling flame, trapping the two tubby friends on the wooden scaffolding.

Looking at each other in silent acceptance, they both leapt hand in hand over the edge of the precipice.

Tim and Julie were falling together as a cobbled heap of man and halfling. Tim knew they were most likely going to die. He only wished he had known how attractive Eliza was to become so he could have pretended to like her back at the Herpides School of Discount Magic, their alma mater of the wizarding arts.

Julie squirmed, struggled, and seemed to be fighting Tim to get a good view of their approaching doom.

This act brought up a wash of past amorous adventures in Tim's mind, but Eliza's blood seeping through Julie's teeth (from the tip of her ear that he soon spat out) reminded Tim that this was not one of those times.

He wished he could have kept… just the tip.

"Owwwwwww!" Tim bellowed as Julie clawed and elbowed all of Tim's precious places, jockeying for a better position of death. "What the hell is wrong with you, Julie?!?" Tim yelled over the roaring sound of the wind becoming trapped on their bulbous forms. Julie managed a mid-air shrug as the entangled pair kept hurtling deeper into the dark.

Not having any idea of his motivation, Tim put Julie's actions behind him for the moment and focused on the task at hand. It turned out he managed to hold onto his staff, so there was a chance they might survive. However, for the life of him, the only thoughts that Tim's mind could conjure were of sticky marshmallow surprises, a halfling delicacy that involved a giant bowl and an over-ambitious serving of soft and rubbery marshmallow mixed with chocolate and any other treats. Suited to the taste of the individual, of course. Tim's personal preference included nougat, caramel sauce, and a smattering of the freshest fruit of the season.

Then in the dark, still far below, Tim could see something glowing.

"Julie, do you see that?" he said.

"Ooh, it's glowy…" Julie responded.

Ah yes, Julie and his competent grasp of the extremely obvious, Tim thought. Searching his mind, he thought of something that might work.

"Hold on to me, you little fool," Tim barked.

Julie for once did not argue and grabbed Tim by his sizable haunches. As he began his incantation, his words once again inexplicably went back to his sticky marshmallow surprise.

"Marshmallow, nougat, and jam!" he bellowed as a soft blue orb of malleable magic encircled the falling pair.

Their velocity immediately dropped, but not fast enough, Tim thought as the glowing at the bottom of the fall still rapidly approached.

Just before impact Tim thought to himself,

"It looks like a forest of dicks."

*A*s awareness slowly crept back to Tim, a dim memory of a colossal phallus rapidly approaching his head and face area seemed to strike a chord. He would have remembered it as another one of those Julie picnic dreams, but this time, he was sure it had been… blue? Why… why… would Tim's mind have made up a giant blue dick? Tim needed to start watching himself. Aurora was what he needed to be thinking about.

Cautiously opening one eye, Tim found that his whole world had become a glowing blue chamber of some sort. It was below him, to each side, and above, except for a Tim-sized hole in what he immediately thought of as the tip. Looking around, Tim did not see Julie anywhere. Carefully lifting himself and checking for broken bones, he looked under his rump to see if the little bastard had been squashed like a bug. Tim was both relieved and disappointed not to find a mangled half-man under him.

But that left the question: where in the realms was he?

Tim stood with a significant amount of effort, then began to try and pat away some of the… blue… that was all over him. He had really blued himself this time, Tim thought. Letting out a bit of a chuckle.

"Tim?" Julie said.

"Julie?" Tim answered.

"Where are you?" Tim asked.

"Outside," Julie answered.

"Outside of what, you dimwitted half-shit?"

Julie didn't answer.

"Julie?" Tim asked again.

"What?" Julie answered petulantly.

"What?!" Tim barked. "Are you seriously pouting right now? You very nearly killed us by attacking that beautiful witch and making us fall off a giant bridge in a ball of fire. I just managed to save us, and now I am stuck in some sort of blue hell, and you have the audacity to pout? I swear to all the gods, I'll put you on a spit and feed your half-link to Leslie myself."

Julie remained quiet for a second, and then Tim began to hear a strange fleshy tapping sound on one of the walls of the member's chamber. After this went on for a few minutes, a small hole appeared, and Julie's awful maw slowly began to suck down the blue flesh of the member until a space was large enough for him to stick his head in. Julie thrust in a sharp stone, and together, the two hewed out a passage large enough for a small cow to pass through… or one obese wizard. Emerging on the other side, Tim realized it really was a forest of blue dicks. The largest and bluest he had ever seen. After a bit of thought, Tim realized they, in fact, were not dicks but were instead a type of giant subterranean mushroom.

Admittedly, this made far more sense than the other.

"Can you see where we fell from?" Tim asked Julie.

"Nope," Julie said as he munched on a large piece of blue mushroom.

"I don't think you... ugh, never mind," Tim said.

The two began to explore their surroundings. The cavern they had fallen from seemed to extend into an equally large canyon on the bottom. The area they were in was relatively flat, interspersed with huge pieces of rock that had fallen from above. The giant blue mushrooms were everywhere and seemed to make up most of the Down Under's ecosystem, at least in this small part. There were other types of mushrooms nearly everywhere. One type seemed to grow exclusively on the walls and was white with strange green spots. Others grew in the shade of the large stones, and a thin, purple type seemed to cluster in groups at the base of the large blue ones. They found no sign of any other types of life apart from a few charred and broken corpses of goblins Eliza must have roasted on the bridge.

There were several tunnels leading off in various directions, but Tim did not want to blindly go off on one of these. If they got lost down here, they would be lost forever, and he was certain his friends were mounting a rescue attempt at this very moment... they were not.

In the end, the pair decided to set up camp in the large blue mushroom that Tim crashed into and were able to make the fungus relatively comfortable. The hole in the top provided an avenue for smoke, and Tim found that he could burn the blue mushroom itself. As the fire started to burn, they turned to the most pressing issue at hand: food.

"How was that blue mushroom on the stomach, Julie?"

Tim asked.

Julie was currently licking the side of the blue mushroom's walls. Tim paused at this and wasn't sure if that was normal behavior or if he was acting odd. Shrugging to himself, Tim decided to take a large piece and hold it over the fire. Maybe that would help disperse anything bad in the mushroom's makeup.

As Tim held his face over the strange blue mushroom smoke, he noticed the walls of the mushroom began to shimmer and shake; it was almost like... uh-oh, too late. Tim suddenly realized he was going on an unexpected psychedelic adventure.

*I*t wasn't that Tim didn't like to do drugs. In fact, under the right circumstances, he genuinely loved them. It was a secret amongst the Halflings of the world actually. Most people thought that the Halflings seemed kind but slow and never seemed too ambitious to change things. In all actuality, they worked extremely hard to make their lives exactly as they wanted. Snug, comfy homes in the ground, an overabundance of food to enjoy, and the most potent of comfort-inducing drugs were all the great staples of a halfling community.

Tim had rarely spent more than a day or two sober in the last century, but those were tried and true strains from people that he trusted; he knew the effects. As the shimmering sensation grew in his mind and body, Tim began to worry a bit less and instead began to wonder what those walls Julie was licking tasted like.

Tim approached a wall, lolled out his tongue, and gave the wall a tentative lick. To his delight, it tasted exactly like sunshine.

Tim and Julie stayed in that state for an unknown amount of time, happily licking the inside of their makeshift camp. But at some point, the novelty wore off, and Tim found that he was impossibly hot.

"Julie, is it warm in here to you?" asked Tim.

Julie nodded and Tim noticed the small halfling cretin was already naked.

"Bastard!" Tim shouted.

"Could've told me," he continued as he disrobed himself.

The next thing Tim noticed was a trail of bright green floaty things that seemed to make a path. As Julie stood there stark naked with a hunk of blue mushroom in his hand, he asked,

"Tim, you see green things?"

Tim, in turn, nodded. Julie took one last mouthful of the blue mushroom and began to trot off down the path, following the green line. Tim decided to follow; there could be treasure at the end of the green road.

Along the way, Tim and Julie had to touch, taste, and smell everything they found, and it was all wonderful. Each of the mushrooms tasted like a different ray of sunshine, and neither of them could get enough. The green line seemed to be their salvation, and Tim decided he trusted it more than anyone or anything.

It showed them mushrooms larger than all the blue ones, even if they were mushed together and tied up like a large blue bouquet that only someone like Leslie or Julie could enjoy. It showed them cracks in the ground that drifted off forever, deeper and deeper, and were covered in a dim red glow. Eventually, the path led Tim and Julie into a series of twisting and narrow caves. It was all Tim could do to squeeze and claw his way ever deeper along the path, but the green one was to be trusted, and Tim would follow. Tim knew he was bleeding, but he didn't care; answers were so close at hand, and he knew at the end of it, he would be embraced by the unending love of a great green being.

After the pair crawled dirty, bleeding, and naked into another large cavern, Tim was met with a true surprise. He found that in all directions, there seemed to be a cavern filled with adorable, small blue dogs. The dogs were strange and walked on two legs, but in Tim's mind, they were so cute that he just wanted to die. Each of them seemed to be wrapped in the green one's energy, so he trusted them implicitly.

The effects of the mushrooms made it so he couldn't quite make out their facial features but could understand some of their gestures. Following them blindly, the little dogs led Tim to a small hole that contained a bed and a big pile of mushrooms.

Tim hadn't noticed what happened to Julie, and honestly, he didn't care. Soon he would be with the green one, and that was all that mattered. As he ate his fill of the mushrooms, he lay down on the most comfortable bed he had ever felt, and at last, he closed his weary eyes and drifted off to a restful and well-deserved slumber.

16

Tim's dreams were truly magical, even for a wizard. The green goddess he imagined appeared to him and took him on a sexual adventure amongst the stars. The goddess introduced him to her sisters, who came in every size, shape, and color, and Tim made love to each of them on every celestial object he could find.

Tim assumed this was his life now and that he would never wake. Reality however, soon came knocking.

One minute, Tim was doing a purple goddess on a small moon, and the next, he was being jabbed awake by something sharp in his guts. As his eyes opened, a world of pain flooded over him. Tim found that his entire body hurt. A thousand tiny cuts covered him. He was dirty and smelled of shit and some other things he couldn't and wouldn't try to identify.

Then, there was the stabbing pain in his gut. As his eyes grew accustomed to the darkness all around him, he found that the pain was not of an internal stimulus but an outside one, and to his horror, he recognized what was causing it. He began shrieking. Yesterday, what had been a painfully cute blue puppy was, in fact, a vicious and flea-bitten kobold. A dog-shaped humanoid known for dwelling deep in the Down Under and for being one of the most violent creatures in the known worlds. Goblins avoided them actively and thought of them as uncivilized monsters. Tim began shaking.

"What do you want?!?" he moaned as the beast jabbed a sharpened stick into Tim's guts over and over again.

The creature didn't answer and, after a time, became bored and walked away. Where the fuck was he and what the fuck happened? Tim knew there was only one thing to do, so he began to cry, loudly.

Tim didn't know how long he sat there crying into the dark, blaming his misfortunes on the world and that dastardly little imp, Julie. For all Tim knew, the kobolds would see Julie as a kindred spirit and make him their king. This made Tim shudder; Julie as an under king would actually be terrifying. This was stopped, however, when out of the dark, a warm piece of not quite solid shit hit Tim square in the face and mouth.

This made Tim cry even louder.

"Will you go on and shut up?" a voice said out of the dark.

Tim wiped the shit out of his mouth as best as he could. He was covered in so much filth he wasn't sure if he could really clean himself up or just sort of move it around a bit.

"Who… who's there?" Tim said, trying to put a bit of steel in his voice but failing horribly.

"A mangy old git who's tired of hearing the squeals and cries of the fattest man I've ever had the displeasure to lay my eyes on."

Tim sat up and began to get a little angry.

"I'm sorry, you bastard, I was just dreaming the greatest life ever, and instead, I found out I am in some sort of prison and probably going to be eaten by a bunch of dog lizards."

The voice just laughed.

"Being eaten by them would be merciful. No, none of us get out of here that easy."

Tim desperately tried not to, but he squealed in fear. At the sound of this, the voice made a defeated sound, and off to Tim's left, a small flame was lit. Tim could suddenly see into the cell adjacent to his, and inside, he saw the most muscular gnome he had ever seen. Well, the only gnome he had ever seen, but he imagined they weren't usually built like that.

"The name's Tink, and if you want to survive in here, little piggy, you better listen to me."

Tink then brought the wayward wizard up to speed. It was fairly normal, in fact, that Tim had never seen a gnome; they generally lived much deeper than even Dwarves and liked it that way. There was less intelligent life down that deep, and Tim learned the Gnomes had a bloodlust for lesser creatures and hunted far and wide to capture rare prey. This is what had led to Tink's capture. He was apparently even more bloodthirsty than your average gnome and had risked coming closer to the surface to try and bag a rare trophy for his village. If he had pulled this off, he said he would have gotten exclusive mating rights for the season and might have gotten to sire many sons.

"Unfortunately, I was lured into a trap, but I killed nearly a dozen of those mangy fleabags, and I would have fucked their corpses too if they hadn't brought me down," bragged Tink.

This made Tim extremely uncomfortable. Actually, he and Julie should meet, Tim thought idly.

"What happened next?" Tim asked, sort of enjoying the story.

"I awoke same as you in this fuckin dirty kennel of the dog beasts. They poked and prodded me for days until I got my first match. You see, piggy, we aren't for eating, well not yet anyway. We are here to fight and to die and then if there's anything left, they eat us."

"Wha… t?" Tim asked, pissing himself right then and there.

Tink tried not to notice Tim actively pissing.

"Yes, we are gladiators of sorts, for sport. They'll come for you eventually. They'll have you tied up and send you into battle, something easy more than like. Maybe a goblin, maybe an underhound. Who knows? My first fight was against a goblin they had caught. I bashed his brains out in the arena and tasted that filth's black blood. To be honest it's not so bad, the fightin' anyway. If I had a better room, I might quite enjoy the entire experience."

Yep, Julie-level psycho, thought Tim. A hundred questions ran through Tim's mind, but he didn't know which to ask first. Muffled barking began to approach the pens, and Tink quickly put out the light.

"Tink?" Tim said.

Tink said nothing, and then Tim heard the door to his own cage open and felt a vice-like rope wrap around his neck. He struggled to scream, but he found it was hopeless. The rope around his neck was tied to a large pole, and it was leading him where they wanted him to go. He was marched through a dim line of cages and caught glimpses of all manner of beasts and men.

Tim was sure he saw a bugbear, a couple of goblins, another gnome, a kobold that was green, a huge spider, and at last, an extremely hairy round shape…

"Julie!" Tim tried to scream.

Julie brought himself up to the side of the cage but didn't speak; he simply waved. Sometimes Julie's dimwit was nice, Tim thought as he approached a growing howl of dozens of dog-like voices. Tim could see a light growing and was thrust into a rock-hewn corridor. The stick left his throat as a door was shut, but the collar remained on.

Without any fanfare, the door on the other side of the corridor opened, and Tim stumbled out into a dirty, lit arena. Hundreds of kobolds filled the stands, mixed with a cadre of other monstrous shapes. Tim didn't have time to scout them all because almost immediately, a door on the opposite side of the arena opened, and through it ran a large naked rat-like pig dog. That was the best his mind could do to describe it: a naked rat pig dog. Maybe this was an underhound? It was obviously built for the Down Under and specifically for the darker parts, Tim suspected. Its eyes were large white orbs that didn't seem to function, and its nose was overly large and sniffed the air wildly, taking in all the strange scents.

"Well, at least it's blind. Should be relatively easy," Tim said to himself.

As soon as he said this the dog looked right at him and began to move in his direction.

"Fuck."

Tim all of a sudden became very aware that he was completely naked. He also noticed that the rat pig dog had very large, sharp front teeth and that its four claws were scooped, probably for digging, but he bet they could also very quickly eviscerate a fat man.

Tim's thoughts ran something like this,

"Fuck fuck fuck fuck fuck fuck, oh fuck fuck fuck fuck."

Just as he was wondering what he could possibly do, one of the dogs standing about the gate threw a sharpened stick at his feet. The dog growled at Tim and showed him his fangs.

"Got it," Tim said to himself.

Thinking as quickly as his near-panic state would allow, Tim grabbed up the stick and ran as far away from the creature as he could. It didn't respond. The beast did turn his head when Tim finally stopped moving. From this limited information, Tim couldn't tell if the creature's hearing worked very well or if it was just actively smelling for him. There wasn't any time to really test and see what it responded to and what it didn't. The thing was large, but it looked as if it hadn't eaten in a while, judging from its protruding ribs. Thinking on his feet, the only way he could really distract it was to make a smell that would be more potent than his already stinking bulk.

Luckily his fight-or-flight response offered him a quick solution. Backing up to the wall, Tim simply eased up the tight grip he had over his own anus, and a flood of fecal matter erupted onto the stone behind him.

The smell was enough that Tim almost vomited on top of it; those blue mushrooms reeked. The kobolds all began to howl and throw bits of trash Tim's way. The rat pig dog had a different response: it immediately began charging at Tim. The creature bowled towards him, but at the last moment, Tim lazily moved towards the left, and the beast struck its head right into the stone where Tim's stinking shit was smeared. As the rat pig dog was stunned, he rammed home the sharp stick into the creature's throat and left it there.

The thing gargled and whined. It was almost pitiful, and if it wasn't for the six-inch incisors sticking out of its mouth, Tim might have felt bad for it.

He had won. What could he say? When he's put in a shitty situation, sometimes he does have the right answer.

As the beast finally died, the door Tim entered from opened, and he retreated without much fuss. The exit door didn't open immediately; instead, Tim felt a loud rumbling rattle on the floor around him. Walking back to the door leading to the arena, he saw a huge stone door open, and out stepped a massive creature.

One of the few classes Tim had enjoyed in school was Beastiality, the study of monsters and men. The thing in front of him was an ogre, a huge cyclopean monster known to wipe out entire villages of any man or beast. Its skin was a sickly see-through color, and it roared at the gathered crowd of kobolds. Tim noticed the stone lip of the arena seemed to have been built with monsters like it in mind, and he saw large scratches etched into the stone.

The ogre marched across the pit, lifting the large dead creature with one dirty hand. Opening its mouth, it swallowed it whole and the sounds of snapping and grinding bones filled the space. The door opposite him in the arena opened again, and out marched five or six well-armed goblins.

Before the fight started, Tim's door was opened, and a large stick once again grabbed a hold of his collar. He was ushered back down to the dark warrens. They took a different path this time, and Tim did not see Julie again.

As he was placed back into his cage, he saw the little gnome light come back on.

"We need to talk, Tim."

"*A* plan?! A fucking plan?!" Tim screamed down at the much smaller gnome as rat pig dog viscera ejected itself off of his quaking naked frame.

"I don't care anything about any fucking plan. I'm naked, I'm tired, I'm covered in the excrement and innards of some sort of mutant rat dog. I am very likely never going to be well rested and fed again before I am literally eaten by monsters. No, Tink. Keep your wasted plans to yourself."

Tink watched as Tim took his considerable naked bulk and curled himself into a disgusting ball of human flesh on the ground. Tink looked away as the shuddering waves of screaming tears shook Tim's ample breasts.

The next day, Tim didn't even have the heart to look over at Tink in the adjacent pen, and for whatever it was worth, Tink gave him the dignity of not speaking to him. His whole body hurt in ways he could have only imagined in some sort of torture universe, and alas, he had none of Aurora's salve to soothe any of his holes. He had thought hiking through the forest was bad, but this, this was something else entirely.

The first thing Tim always did in the morning was take a piss. Though, this time, it was different. He was still naked, of course, and covered in a film of various muds and bodily fluids, some that were his own and some that were not. No, the difference about today was that at the end of his still large and sagging gut, he saw a very small yet familiar tip sticking out.

"What in the gods' names is this fucking thing now?" Tim said to himself.

His first instinct was a leach, or some sort of horrid growth, had taken up residence there, or maybe that old infection was rearing its ugly head, but taking a second look, in his panic, Tim realized that the small, wrinkled tip before him was the head of his own penis.

Gods, how long had it been since he saw that little guy with his own two eyes? Sixty, seventy years maybe? Who knew that through such horror and anguish, he would get to see his own penis again. The world was funny like that sometimes, Tim thought to himself as the dribble from his now visible penis dripped on his drawn-up ball sack.

Tim stood there for a long time, admiring the strange patterns of wrinkles, thinking of all the strange adventures that they had taken together—and for its part, had taken them blindly. His ruminations were interrupted by Tink, who finally decided to jump in on the now awake wizard.

"Getting the long and short of it, are ye, Tim? Looks mostly short to me," Tink said, laughing.

"Shut up, you skinny dwarf," Tim said with bitter sarcasm in his words.

It wasn't that short. Just slightly below the human average.

Quite respectable really.

"DWARF?!" Tink shrieked and walked away from the wall close to Tim's cell.

"And that makes two wins for me this morning. I thank you," Tim mumbled to himself as he sat down on the least filthy part of his little personal dungeon.

Where had he gone wrong? He and Julie should have died inside of Kim's hole like he was always destined to do. It would have been either a food- or sex-related accident or maybe both at once if it hadn't been for the goblins, and even then, that was a fair bet.

But no, he had been so concerned with protecting his laziness and that godforsaken worn-out hole that he had lost everything, even his chance for a swiftish death. Now, who knows when and how it would happen. He would simply have to endure this. Gods, but how?

Tim steeled himself to his new life and settled into his new routine. He was thrown some sort of slop to eat every day or so. Once a week, sometimes twice, he would be dragged out of his cage and made to fight in front of the blue dog creatures.

So far, he continued to win, and his deep and personal desire to never die tired. He just wanted to be comfortable one more time in his life. In his spare time, when he wasn't stress sleeping, he would sit in his cage and stare farther and farther down his taint as his receding gut slowly exposed it to him. It was like reading a book from his childhood, each mark a cherished memory.

That all changed, though. After a few weeks, Tim began to notice that many of his soft feminine curves were now being re-placed by angular wedges of solid flesh. He assumed they were all tumors. Maybe that would alleviate his suffering.

They came for him early one morning. He hadn't even got to

suck any fresh slop off the ground.

"Pipe down, you demented puppies. I'm coming, I'm coming," Tim said as the small blue dog men prodded him with their sharp sticks.

Tim liked to imagine that they were blue because they had once been too fond of blueberries and that if he were to ever leave this place, he would like to take at least one of them with him, chop them up, and have a nice cobbler. Kobold cobbler: best case, it was a dessert dish; worst case, it was a Down Under meat pie. Either way, he wins.

The dogs pushed Tim down his usual parade ground, past all the other shit-covered cages of various sentient and non-sentient beings, each giving it all to either die or survive another day in this carnival from hell, but with no deep-fried treats to be seen.

Then there he was, thrown naked through the gate once again, and all around him stood a cheering crowd of the ugliest bunch of monsters Tim had ever seen gathered in one place. The smell was overwhelming, even for someone who was literally covered in a half inch of their own feces and several different species' blood and various juices.

Tim expected to see the opposing gate open immediately and some new horror rush out to meet him, but nothing happened.

Then horror struck the confused man-child. On the dais, where a large and fat dog usually sat, another strange creature arose in his place. It was Julie.

"My dear Julie," Tim said with a smile breaking across his shit-stained lips.

This smile was like one ray of bright warmth on a dark winter's day, and it was covered immediately by darkness. Tim could see the finery of the clothes that Julie now wore, and he could also see a simple leash bound to Julie at his hip. The leash was attached to two female dogs, and he was… he was smiling.

"Julie," Tim said again, the anger and betrayal growing inside him like those tumors.

How did this happen? Tim was living a life of a gladiator, and Julie was all dressed up in nice clothes and banging bitches? This was unfathomable.

Tim was about to mention Julie's weight or maybe make a jab about his hairline. He knew both of those caused Julie quite a bit of social distress, but before he could yell it out, the gate on the other side of the arena opened, and out stepped a very ugly and very large creature. It was a bugbear, and Tim peed more than a little bit.

Bugbears were like Goblins except much bigger, not quite an ogre, but sizable enough to easily turn a naked wizard into lunch. This was bad. The only weapon Tim had was the jealousy burning in his guts like any girl on prom night. He would make Julie pay.

The bugbear let out a roar and charged him, swinging his tree trunk like a club in swift circles of destruction. Tim thanked the blue mongrels for the workout routine and starvation because he found that he was able to move out of the way of the creature's wild and powerful swings. A month ago, he would've been dead.

Rolling from one blow to the next, Tim began to look around and decide what he could do to stop this monster from eating him, backside first, in what would most likely be his last ass-to-mouth adventure. Most of his fights so far had been relatively easy; some sort of blind or fat creature without too many weapons would be sent against him, and Tim would give it a stab or two with his stick and call it a day.

Tim thrust out at the bugbear with his sharpened stick. He made good contact at the back of the creature's right knee, and with a gut-softening crunch, Tim saw his sad little stick break against the creature's thick skin. In his moment of surprise, Tim also caught a strong backhand slap from the beast and tumbled back and away and crashed against the rough stone wall.

The dog men bayed with delight, and Tim even caught a glimpse of a smiling Julie with one hand each on the disgusting blue bitches at his side. Tim thought it was over as he saw the bugbear triumphantly shaking his trunk to the stands of cheering monsters.

Tim struggled to his feet, and as he did, a spear struck the ground in front of him. It wasn't just a sharpened stick this time either; it was a proper-looking spear, and according to a distant memory from Herpides School of Discount Magic in Tim's over-adrenalized mind, it was of elven make to boot. A weapon of the first empire.

Where this came from and why were interesting questions Tim would like answered, but this was not the time or place for them. As the big bugbear turned around and saw the spear, it roared and charged Tim again.

Tim did a roll that definitely hurt something in his back and picked up the spear. His arms and hands seemed to have a mind of their own as they presented the spear horizontally above his head in a blocking motion. Tim had just enough time to think to himself that this was going to break all the bones in his arms (and then kill him) when the great swing hit. To his surprise, the spear stopped the blow cold.

Tim, the crowd, and the bugbear all sort of just stopped in surprise at the block. Somehow gathering his senses back first, Tim swung the spear out again, seemingly by its own will, and delivered a hammer blow across the bugbear's face.

The beast howled and stumbled back, raising one of its massive paws to cover the gashing wound on its cheek.

"What the fuck is happening?" Tim said as the spear spun like a top in his untrained fingers.

The bugbear began to look scared. Tim knew that look. It was the same one Julie got when he heard another sheep was missing and they suspected foul play. Tim paused at that. But the thought was lost again when the bugbear swung his tree trunk back at Tim.

Again, the spear met the trunk, and again, it checked its advance.

The fight continued like this, with the bugbear giving Tim more and more room until, at last, it was out of the spear's reach. After circling like this for several minutes, the spear began to grow warm in Tim's sweaty hands. Tim thought this was odd until the heat became unbearable. As he was going to drop it with a curse, his arm cocked back, and he was compelled to yell the word for fire in his arcane tongue.

"Oatmeal crisps!" were the words that actually came out of his mouth, but Tim knew that his magic wasn't the real catalyst behind what happened next.

As the words left his lips, so did the spear leave his hand, alight in white flames, launching itself at the huge beast. The creature had nowhere to go as the spear passed through its face and stuck itself deep in the surrounding wall with the now detached head decorating its bloody shaft. Tim did not know what to do but slowly raised his hand as a sign of victory.

The dogs went wild.

After the crowd settled down, a pair of guard dogs came, but instead of ushering him out, they took him to a penned-in section of the arena seating and allowed him to watch. They even brought him some cooked meat.

"Must be the winner's circle," Tim muttered to himself as

we watched a team of dogs try to remove the elven spear from the wall below.

They eventually gave up and Tim began to look around as he waited for a new match to start. Tim saw ogres, kobolds, goblins, and even a few of the dreaded chinchilladads, those most dreaded of creatures from the legendary southern jungles. They sat, wrapped in dark hoods, and even from a distance, Tim could hear the evil chittering and chattering of their bucked front teeth.

As his eyes continued to wander over one creature and then another, Tim finally found who he had sought all along, Julie.

Julie was doing his best not to make eye contact, and from this level, Tim could see that he, indeed, was living a life of splendor. Four kobold bitches, clearly in heat, were pawing at his short and stubby appendages. A great pelt of some sort of exotic undercreature draped his shoulders, and each of Julie's fat little fingers was wrapped in a ring of precious gems.

"What in the name of cream of milk is going on?!" Tim exclaimed.

As he was getting ready to yell obscenities at the obese halfling, Tim saw a group of wild men approach Julie. They greeted him with some deference, and Julie allowed them to sit. At that moment, Tim saw Julie pull a most remembered book from the folds of his cape.

"Oh, broccoli no!" Tim bellowed and began to rattle the cage around him.

As Tim began to shriek, he saw some commotion happening in the arena below him; the spear was shaking itself from the wall and had interrupted the beginning of the new bout. Several goblins, some green and some blue, stopped fighting one another and instead focused on trying to grab hold of the fine elven weapon. As it came free from the wall, it eluded all the small grasping claws and made a beeline for Tim's cage.

Once again, the small and underworked lizard part of Tim's brain obeyed the commands of the freewheeling weapon; instead of cowering in fear, he simply reached for it. Just as Tim was about to feel the luscious tip in his fingers, a huge crushing blow struck Tim's thick skull, and darkness enveloped him.

Tim was dreaming of soft and supple chocolate balls. A little sweet, a little salty, and big on the comfort factor. Tim had made them so many times before he could just feel the light tracing on the back of the recipe. It had been very intricate. Julie was good at finding the best quality paper for Tim's recipe book.

Another salty ball hit Tim in the mouth. Gasping in delight, Tim took a small bite. He instantly woke up screaming.

Tim did not take the time to see where he was; he would stop at nothing to get that horrid taste from his mouth. He jumped up and ran around, scraping his fingers across his white forested tongue in an effort to physically remove the foul-tasting intruders. As he danced and screamed in horror, he heard the almost melodic laughing of one small dastardly gnome.

"Tink!" Tim screamed.

Tink was very nearly openly weeping with delight at this point.

"Tim, oh gods, Tim. It went right in… it went right in your mouth. And then, and then to damn it all, you started eating it. Ha! Oh, my short gods. I would… I wouldn't have believed it."

Tim was shaking and had found a small wedge of bone on the ground that he was now using to scrape his tongue and teeth as well as he could manage.

"What is it?" he asked with an expression that said he already knew. In his heart, he knew.

Tink continued laughing.

"Say it, Tink. Dammit Tink, say it!"

"It was a little piece of shit!" Tink said with a bellowing laugh, showing Tim his fingers very close to each other.

Tim looked down at where he had been sleeping—or had he passed out? No matter that, he thought as he took in the small piles of shit balls that outlined where his slightly lessened bulk had been.

"Gods, Tink, how long have you been throwing your shit at me?" Tim looked at him with a more serious expression.

"Several days now," Tink responded with a blank stare in his eyes.

Tim reached up and touched what he now realized was a bandage-wrapped head.

"What the hell happened to me? Last thing I remember was being in the arena, and then I saw… I saw that fucking snake, Julie, and he had… he had my book! That devious vegetable eater!"

Tink nodded and assumed this book was very important since Tim was a wizard.

"What was he doing with your book?" Tink asked, rolling up something between his gnomey little fingers.

"It looked like he was showing it to the filth in the arena, Tink! They had the look of wild men, maybe from the border of the great ice. Julie has obviously been using it to increase his status. It's incredibly valuable, Tink. There's no telling what sort of trouble he could get in unless we stop him."

"Good," said Tink.

"Good?" replied Tim.

"Yes, my rotund friend. Now you have a reason to get out of this place, and that mark on your noggin makes me think of one of our first steps."

Tim rubbed his head; he wasn't going to like this.

Tink was trained to act as a commander of gnomish forces against the might of horrible underworld monsters and legions of other ilk that they sometimes faced. It shook him to his core that he had only one fat and criminally unintelligent wizard as a soldier, but that would have to do.

"Well, Tim, now that you are on board, we have the beginnings of a plan. We have many obstacles before us, but on the other side lies the sweet, sweet freedom of the Down Under's depths and the opportunity for me to bed many a fair gnomish lass. If we escape, and you please me, I could see you settling in as a… worker in our fields maybe… But either way, you wouldn't have to live here anymore. We Gnomes don't senselessly give away our lives for the entertainment of others. Instead, we engage in one-on-one combat for GLORY!

"There is no comparison here. Now, using my tactical

genius and about a year of personal free time, I have outlined the problems that lie between us and freedom.

"Number 1: These cages are too strong for us to break out of on our own. They may look flimsy, but the bone is made up of some sort of magical creature; my first guess would be an under dragon, but that is beside the point. Someone on the outside will have to help us, either intentionally or unintentionally.

"Number 2: Once we are out, you can bet your wrinkled pecker those dogs will start howling and come at us with everything they've got. Now, once I have a blade, I can take on more than my fair share, but you… Well, you seemed worthless until that elven weapon decided to bond with you. Now…"

"Wait, what?" Tim interrupted.

"Before that spear attached itself to you, you were pretty much worthless," Tink said.

"Attached to me?" Tim replied in a disbelieving tone.

Tink rolled his eyes.

"Tim, you're not so daft as to think that YOU, of all creatures, all of a sudden became a master spearman?"

"Well, I…"

"No. No. No. No. YOU most certainly did not. You're a bloody wizard, Tim. Do you know nothing of elven weapons?" Tink barked.

"Well, I… I focused on other scholarly pursuits."

Tink rolled his eyes again.

"OK. Well, as any gnomish child knows. The two oldest races of mostly good stock are the Elves and Dwarves. These peoples have a broader access to magic than most other races. This also includes their crafting abilities. Is any of this ringing a bell?" Tink asked while making a clock motion with his hands.

Tim answered by staring at him blankly.

"Continuing on, while dwarven weapons are known for enchantments of great power like adding lighting or fire to a weapons attack, the Elves were able to imbue their weapons with something like the soul of its wielder."

"A soul?" Tim said.

"Yes, Tim, a soul or its experience or something. The greatest elven warriors were able to put enough of themselves into their weapons, so if they fell in battle, they could continue to fight on. Now, these weapons are extremely picky and almost fight for no one, especially a non-elf. How the gods chose you, well it hurts to think."

"So, this weapon chose me, and it's like my slave now?" Tim said.

Tink hit himself.

"No, you big fat bloody fool. It's chosen to let you wield it, making you a force to be reckoned with as long as it finds you worthy. It can fall silent whenever IT chooses, not you. Does any of this make sense?"

Tim nodded vaguely, thinking of how cool it would make him look to those gnomish women Tink was always going on about. Maybe he would rule the Gnomes.

"But I don't get it," Tim said. "How does the spear help us? Where is it?"

Tink smiled.

"**F**uck Julie, Fuck Tink, Fuck blue dogs, Fuck goblins, fuck everyone and everything."

This was the new mantra Tim mumbled each and every day as he was required to fight more and more often in the kobold arena. Unfortunately, these blue cretins had not given Tim back his new magic spear, and he had to actually learn how to survive.

The dogs had imprisoned his spear above the main viewing area of the arena in thick goblin-hewn iron bars. Each time Tim fought, the spear would strain against its bars for the duration of the fight. This had caused great interest amongst the denizens of dog town at first, but now they just saw it as a matter of course. Tim and Tink were the only ones who noticed the spear was slowly carving away at its restraints.

For the escape plan to work, they were going to need that spear and a couple of other things that Tim dreaded even more than that.

Sitting in the "box" was what he did after every fight, and it was here that he got to see a bit more of the other combatants. He found this somewhat interesting, but mainly his thoughts dwelled on his hatred of Tink and of the most dreaded Julie. Tim wanted to pound those two. No, he wanted to grind them. If only there was a way for Tim to grind multiple men at once. Tim sighed, maybe one day.

Most of his time in the box was spent staring down Julie, who did not have the good graces to even look at him. Each day, Julie seemed to be more and more comfortable in dog town as his wealth seemed to grow. Today, Julie was visited by some of the desert men from across the elven gulf. Tim had always read they rode humped beasts across the great deserts; he wondered if that was true. His wonderings stopped with a great lump when Tim saw Julie take out the recipe book and tear another precious page out of it.

Tim's guts wept.

As Tim continued to make weeping sounds from his box, the great stone door rolled open, and out stepped the arena champion. About fifteen feet tall, easily over a ton in weight, this beast of an ogre had the biggest vagina Tim had ever seen. However, what disturbed him the most was the way she scratched it as she looked at him. Why not cover that thing up? Today the scratching was stopped before a climax thanks to the swift intervention from a group of centaurs who were poked and prodded out into the arena. Tim had never seen them before. With the bodies of large horses and the torsos of something like men, they were a mysterious people who lived on the great plains west of the human kingdoms. Tim thought they looked magnificent.

As each and every one of them was shredded piece by piece by the great ogre, though, Tim wished he had never seen one.

After the fight, Tim saw the spear had worked out a bit more wiggle room. Luckily, Tim was ushered out as the Great Giant commenced its energetic scratching routine. He was taken back to his cell, and he plopped himself down on the bit of earth he thought of as his bed. Tim began to recite the recipe for apple turncake when he heard the sound of the bard a few cages down.

There once was a wizard named Tim,
who lived in a grand hole named Kim.
He had no wife, nor kids or a life.
He slept and he smoked and enjoyed a good poke.
The happiest of wizards named Tim.

Tim's comfort and bulk, he never did sulk
As he loved his life of laze.
He cooked and he dreamed,
and with Julie, he creamed
The creamiest of pies in his days.

Then one fateful day, it was dashed.
His hole Kim had been turned to ash.
In one fell swoop, his life turned to poop,
And he could no longer sit on his ass.

Now Tim, the great wizard, is all but bewildered.
His stamina withered and broke.
His hole and his comfort, a dream that has suffered,
Has all gone away up in smoke.

"What the fuck was that for?" Tim asked.

"I'm sick of your fucking recipes and your fucking whining. You stupid wizard!" the bard barked.

This caused Tink to laugh out very loudly.

"Shut up, Tink," Tim said, sick of everyone.

Tink laughed again.

"Eh, Tim," he said with a cough, "this is Randall Tip-tongue. I've invited him to join our little party."

Tim sat down and had a bit of a cry.

"What good will a bard do?"

"Good? What good can I do, you ask? I am Randall Tip-tongue, bard to kings, servicer of queens. I have written ballads that have caused many maids to drop their dresses on the spot and men to offer me their wives. I, sir, am crucial to this escape."

Tim rolled his eyes.

"Tink, if you want to get laid, I am almost to the point where I would give you some action as long as you promise to kill me afterwards."

Tink approached his bars.

"I am not the one who will be getting some, Tim," he said with a wink.

"Oh gods," muttered Tim.

*T*he next day, Tim stood shaking in the arena. Tink and Randall had each thrown whatever bodily waste and old food they had handy into his cell and encouraged Tim to cover himself with as much of it as possible.

Tim had never loathed himself more than now.

The reasoning for the stink had been Tink's idea. According to him, he had actually tracked and killed an ogre or two himself, and apparently, female ogres are attracted to two things: bulk and stink.

Tim's bulk had been rapidly shrinking, but he was by no means a thin man yet, and his stink, well, his stink was approaching legendary status. It was because of this smell that Tink believed the great female ogre had started to initiate a bit of a mating ritual with Tim. Tink's plan was going to ensure that Tim embraced this stink even more in an attempt to lead the old girl on a bit.

As Tim tried to think of more ways to sexually interest the great beast, a loud voice suddenly spoke in his mind.

"That's the most disgusting thing I have ever heard someone think before, Tim."

Tim's face quickly ran through what he imagined must have been a host of emotions as the words still seemed to hang in his mind. As he continued to spin and look for its source, he heard a very loud sigh in his mind.

"Up here, idiot," the very proper voice said.

Tim looked straight up.

"No, no, over here on the wall. How many magical objects are you bound to!?"

Tim slowly panned around the arena, his eyes finally fixing on the elven spear.

"Bingo, you great hairless ape."

"You can talk?" Tim asked.

"I'm sorry, did I not bind with a magic wielder? Are you a hedge mage, perhaps?" questioned the spear.

Tim coughed,

"No, no. I am a classically and tower-trained wizard."

"Could have fooled me."

"I'm just a bit rusty, well, on everything."

"I can see that, and as you can see, if I stay up here much longer, I will be rusty myself!" the spear said, laughing to itself.

Tim let out a nervous chuckle.

"So, are you really going to do it?" asked the spear in Tim's mind.

"Do what?" Tim asked, genuinely curious.

"Since we've bonded, I have been privy to every sick thought in that pitiful pink mind of yours. Tim, are you going to try and seduce that ogre?"

Tim nodded.

"Thank the gods most of my people are dead," the spear said seriously.

"Well, you know why we need it, don't you?"

"Yes, yes, the bone cages and what all. I could just pop from this wall now, and we could try and kill the lot, not have to watch you die sinking yourself lower than anyone has ever sunk before."

Tim let out a large gulp. After a few more minutes, Tim was able to talk Shafty out of leaping from the wall and going out in a blaze of glory.

Yes, the spear wanted to be called Shafty.

Instead, Shafty agreed to wait until Tim tried out his plan and then he could improvise if needed. As this agreement was loosely agreed to, the large stone door opened, and out stepped the huge and sexually frustrated ogre. Upon seeing Tim, she marched right for him at a sexual saunter, which was even more disturbing than it sounds. Tim could have sworn he saw some of her parts stiffen and nod at him.

"Cursed turnips," Tim muttered to himself.

Tim didn't know how Tink had gotten the dogs to agree to a team fight with Tim and the ogre, but he sure as hell hated him for it. The large beast was already starting to leave a snail trail from behind her overly excited loins, and Tim couldn't help but think that they had all overdone it with the stink. She was too attracted to him.

As she was about to reach for him, the opposing gate opened, and out rushed a veritable army of anthropodans. Anthropodans are large ant-like beings with some traits of upright two-legged creatures blended into their insect anatomy. They are strong, violent, and are some of the most dreaded creatures in the Down Under.

Tim had never been so relieved in his life.

The fight could only be characterized in one way, for in a world full of staggeringly large disappointments, this one took the cake and the recipe book down with it. In the ogre's sexual rage, she barely even noticed the ant men. With a few fell swoops, she scooped them up and bashed their bodies again and again against the stone wall of the arena, the whole time making disturbing eye contact with Tim.

Tim pissed himself, which only hastened the ogress's appetite.

When the fight was over, the small entryway Tim had entered through opened, and he made a run for it. For every ten of his steps, he could hear one big loping wet step of the ogress, and she was gaining on him fast. He had just reached the door when he heard a thunderous roar, a bellow from the giant as she smashed her fists against the wall behind him.

Tim turned to see an army of kobolds coming to try and restrain the she-beast. Gods, he hoped they could hold for a few minutes. His guards took him back to his cell, and even from there, he could hear her lamenting howls.

"Went well, did it?" Tink asked with a shit-eating grin

across his face.

"What do you think?" Tim said, honestly more scared now than he had ever been.

As he uttered the words, a stone-splitting crack shook the city, and he knew she was out.

Tim couldn't do much but wait as the sounds of screams and crashes grew louder. As the she-beast breached the prison floor, moaning with anticipation, she flattened walls and prisoners with ease. Randall the bard was a fortunate casualty.

Then at the apex of her lusty rage, she found herself at the bars of Tim's cell... mere inches from her prize.

Now most don't know this, as it is a peculiar thing to try and study, but the mating rituals of Ogres are a very interesting topic. The females of the species have an overwhelming sex drive. That, paired with their strength, often leads them to seek out the strongest-smelling males and try to assert their dominance over them to satisfy their desires. Of course, this is generally a welcome action by male ogres, who tend to return the aggression with a *growing arousal.*

However, Tim was not a male ogre, and as he watched the beast breach through the wall of his cell, he was unfortunately not able to *"return the aggression with the growing arousal"* that the female ogre had expected by his smell.

Though not to be dissuaded, the ogress grabbed Tim by the right arm and flipped him over on his back. She crouched over him and began to insert the entirety of his arm, which happened to be roughly the same size as an average male ogre's member, into her gaping nether regions in a rhythmic pulsing fashion.

"Hoolllyyy carrot sticks!!!! Why is this happening to meee?!?!?!" Tim screamed.

As Tim was panting in despair at being literally arm fucked by the ogre, Tink tentatively watched as she had her way with Tim.

"Hellllpp!!" exclaimed Tim in a muffled terror, having now been flipped on his stomach in what was a new position even for the experienced Tim.

What seemed like an eternity passed as the ogre bent and molded Tim every which way to achieve her pleasure needs. Completely helpless, Tim mimicked a dying antelope and went limp in surrender and shock, effectively choosing the *"flight"* option in the fight-or-flight quandary.

Mentally, he escaped the situation and focused all brainpower on remembering his happy place. For a brief moment, he was transported back to the warm comfort of Kim's hole. He sat in his comfiest of chairs, puffing the strongest of herbs from his favorite pipe, thumbing through his vast collection of pie recipes, and planning for which ingredients he would send Julie off to retrieve. As he lost himself in the memory of this, while his left arm was elbow deep inside the female ogress's vagina, he felt for the first time in weeks a semblance of contentment and happiness.
About another half hour passed before the ogress tired herself out. Once finished, she tossed Tim to the side like a used tissue and ran off into the distance.
Tink looked at Tim, and he even felt bad for him.

"My gods, Tim. I… I uhh… I'm sorry," Tink said, lowering his head.

Tim was still somewhere else. He was drenched from head to toe, and there was a taste and smell permeating his entire being. As he came back to reality, in a shell shock, he looked over at the ruin of Randall's cell and felt immediate jealousy that the bard had been crushed so completely before it all got started.

Tim sat up, squelching as he did; his whole body was a slippery mess. As he found his bearings, Shafty managed to wring loose and fly out from the direction of the arena, placing itself against a brace of the bone Tim was leaning on.

"Hi there, stranger," Shafty said telepathically.

Tim did not answer. He just reached out and grabbed Shafty by the shaft and was happy he had someone to hold. Tink picked through the rubble of what had been their prison and came up with a pair of rough kobold swords.

"Well, Tim, do you want to leave straight away? Or are you set on finding that book of cookies you are always mewling about?" Tink asked.

Tim gripped Shafty even harder.

"Let's go get that halfling traitor," he said as he placed Shafty onto his back.

21

With Tink in the lead, the trio set off to find Julie in the chaos that the now sexually satisfied ogress had unleashed. It looked like, in her haste to reach Tim, she had destroyed half of the city, and now she was still rampaging as the dogs would not allow her to have her post-sex nap. It was an excellent cover.

They ran into little trouble on their way to the blue lizard dogs' major residential area — but Tink did strike down a few passers-by just for good fun.

Tim didn't care a lick; all of them should burn for what had happened to him.

A large group of dogs were gathering in what could loosely be described as a plaza surrounded by sizable residential structures constructed from stone and salvaged wood. The howling of the city was nearly unbearable. As they ran down a bone-strewn alleyway, Tink pushed Tim into a doorway and placed his hand over his mouth.

"What the —" Tim started.

"Give me a second," Tink said, looking at his hand disgustedly and trying to wipe what he had found there on his pants.

With that, Tink dashed off down a separate alleyway, leaving Tim alone with his disturbing thoughts.

"Would you mind not thinking so loudly, Tim?" Shafty asked politely in Tim's mind.

"Shafty, I was just sexually assaulted with the force of a genocidal event. How can I not think about it?" Tim retorted.

"Good point. Maybe this will help," thought Shafty in return.

Instantly, Tim's mind was taken across a thousand battlefields and ten thousand deaths, each one focusing on the combatants' eyes as life left them. When Tim came back around, he was screaming, and Tink was shaking him as hard as he could.

"Whoa… calm down there, big fella. We have work to do," Tink said and pointed at a small and clearly pregnant kobold he had captured.

"Jesus, these things are even uglier up close," Tim said, examining the creature closely.

"Ruck off," the bitch hissed and nipped at Tim's outstretched fingers.

"Holy hot pies! I don't think since I've been down here, I've heard these little bastards speak," Tim exclaimed.

Tink nodded and said,

"They can talk, just don't really care to. They say a lot

with scent glands and body language; they are mostly beasts after all."

The kobold answered with a menacing growl.

"Calm down, calm down, shit for breath," Tink said and made a calming gesture with his outstretched sword. "My buddy and I just want a bit of information."

The dog looked nervously around the alley and seemed to come to the decision that it didn't really have any other choice.

"R-okay," the dog said. "What do you want?"

"We ar—" Tink started.

"I want to know where that thieving sexual deviant blueberry-looking fuck is!" Tim shouted, getting closer than he meant to the kobold's sharp teeth.

"Ris that all?" she answered. "He has lain with all the kobolds in town. I think my pups are his," she said, indicating the large bump on her belly. "He's in the house with the columns. Traded for it."

"You don't care what we do to him?" Tink asked.

The kobold shook her head. Tink was about to usher her out of the alley when Shafty's shaft protruded from her chest just below the sternum. Shock crossed her face as she died, and Tink tried to wipe the arterial spray off of his face and chest.

"What the fuck, Tim??" Tink screamed.

"Can you imagine if one of those fucking pups got out of here Tink? It would be a monster like the world has never seen before. We will need to burn this whole town to ash if we can," Tim replied matter of factly.

Tink was surprised but, after thinking about it for a second, seemed to agree with the deranged wizard. The pair continued their silent run down through the closely packed alleyways of the kobold residential section until, at last, they came upon the large columned house that the bitch had mentioned before. Out of all the kobold structures, this was the first one that seemed to be made of actual wood and worked stone. Before Julie traded for it, it must have belonged to one of their chiefs or some sort of other evil dignitary.

As they approached, a pack of pregnant dogs ran from the house and out into the street.

Tink leapt to work and struck most of them down before they could get very far. With a boost from Tim, Shafty took care of the rest. Tim knew it was dark work but felt strongly that the world was a bit safer for it.

The two companions pushed in the large wooden door and entered the two-story structure. Tim was fucking livid.

He had spent the last month—maybe two—living in a shit-floored prisoner cage, mostly naked and usually covered in at least the fluids and waste of himself and one other creature. He had lost weight, he had fought to the death a dozen times, and this little bitch… this little bitch right here had been living in a house that was almost as nice as Kim's hole? The fucking audacity of it. Tim saw comfy chairs and blankets around every corner. The downstairs seemed to consist primarily just of a large kitchen and nap area. Tim couldn't fucking believe it.

"Nice place," said Tink, eyeing a pair of wall-mounted swords.

Then from the back stair, a familiar voice said,

"Hello, Tim."

22

"You... you plump bastard!"

Tim screamed as Julie sauntered his rotund form down the stairs. It was only after he took a few more steps that Tim saw that his cape had a train and that two female kobolds were holding the ends of it for him as he descended the stairs.

Before Julie could reply, Tim heard Shafty screaming incoherently in his mind. He reached out, but he found the spear had shut him out... or itself off. Tim looked puzzled.

"I have grown even softerer here, Tim. I have tasted delicacies and other things your myopic mind couldn't believe or even begin to process."

As Julie said this, he made a summoning motion with his index finger and stroked under the chin of one of the dogs. Tim grimaced.

"You, Tim... look... bad. Like farmer or outside person.

Your body looks like you've been lifting like a mason or a wood choppy," continued Julie.

Tim didn't know why, but this hurt his feelings. He had lost quite a bit of weight, and the constant fighting to the death had toned him up a bit. This was stupid; Julie insulting him for being healthier was no reason to start fighting. He was here for a reason.

"You two girls can scissor later with these pups if you like, but we are here for the book, mate," Tink said, looking menacing with both his swords still drawn.

"Food hoarder!" Tim said and pointed his finger at Julie.

"Book… make Julie big man. It's mine. I find all pretty paper to begin with!" Julie replied.

"But I found all the recipes… well, most of them any-way!" Tim shrieked.

"Recipes?" Tink asked.

"Well, uh, yes… it's a book of my…"

Julie coughed. Tim finished,

"…our favorite recipes, which were all painfully curated over the years. You can't put a value—"

"I'm leavin'," Tink said and walked out the still-open front door.

"Give it!" Tim barked, holding out his calloused hand.

"No," Julie said in a high-pitched voice similar to an an-gry toddler.

"Julie…" Tim warned.

"Julie have best life with books and dogs," he replied, his tone growing softer.

"I've seen that," Tim said and let out a huge sigh.

"Were our recipes really that popular? It was almost like that restaurant idea we had, The Horny Dragon…"

"They came from everywhere for papers. They liked the backs more than the fronts. Just like me. At first, I going to save Tim and leave… but Julie likes it even better here now. I respected!" Julie said, beaming.

"The backs?" Tim was puzzled and held out his hand for the book again.

Reluctantly, Julie held it out, and Tim could see the sorry state his life's work was now in. She was beaten, battered, torn, and plundered. Seeing it in such a state sent Tim back to how Kim's hole had looked the last time he had seen it. Ah, to delve into her once again, he could almost feel her warmth as he gripped Shafty's girth. It would be like coming home.

But that sense of knuckle-deep warmth was quickly stolen from Tim, much like his sweet hole, Kim.

The recipe book was in such a sorry state, he almost dared not look through it. His oldest recipe, double grease fried sandwich, was gone, and the one after that, and the one after that, his favorite cookie recipe… and gods, had they even left… no! He quickly skipped to the middle and bellowed in pain; it was gone. He dropped the book and had a good sob right there on the floor.

"Why, Julie? Why did you do this to me? Was I not a good and somewhat lenient master all these years? I always let you have my leftovers, whether it was women or food. Why did you leave me so low? And the book…"

Tim looked at Julie then and saw the little monster seemed to be struggling with something and might actually be sorry for what it had done.

"Well, friend?" Tim said, trying to capitalize on the moment.

"Julie sorry, Tim. Jealous of Tim's eyes, always looking at Leslie. Soon she would mount Tim like Julie used to."

Tim didn't have a response because, gods, how could he? What the fuck was he blabbering on about? Leslie mounting him? And he used to?!?

"Julie, there are so many things that you just said that I honestly don't fucking understand. But I am going to presume that you are saying you are jealous of our new friends?"

Julie nodded down at his ham-sized swollen feet.

"So out of your jealousy, you let me be beaten, tortured, and treated as an armed combatant while you feasted and fucked your way to a new pants size. All because you were jealous?"

Julie nodded again.

"That's super fucked up."

Tim was thinking about how to respond when he was suddenly interrupted by Shafty saying,

"Turn that page back over."

"What?" Tim said out loud.

"What?" replied Julie.

"No, not you," Tim said, looking down over his shoulder at Shafty.

"Nobody else here, Tim," Julie said, looking worried that maybe Tim had finally lost it.

"No, no, the spear talks," Tim said hurriedly.

Julie seemed to have decided something and said,

"Of course, master. I talk to lots of things. Sometimes even nose treasures. We will…"

Tim stopped listening as Shafty's voice rang in his head again:

"Turn to the back of the page now, you fat idiot!"

In protest of the rather rude language, Tim opened the book again and glanced at the back of the first page.

"It's backwards, you imbecile!" Shafty telepathically shouted at Tim.

Tim sent his thoughts to Shafty and indicated that it most certainly wasn't backwards; this was his book after all.

"DO IT, DO IT NOW!" the spear shrieked in his mind.

As he did, something on what he had thought of as the back clicked and Tim flipped the book over. Rubbing his always moist fingers, Tim scratched away a bit of bodily filth and could make out a word.

"Forb. What's a 'forb'?" Tim asked.

Julie sat down immediately to have a good think on the subject. Almost as suddenly he answered,

"Is it an orb that you f—"

"Forbidden," Shafty said.

A cold grip grabbed Tim's heart when he heard the word, and he honestly hoped it was a heart attack. Tim gulped,

"Forbidden?"

"Open it," Shafty said again.

Tim did as he was told and flipped to the first page that wasn't torn. On the other side was Tim's recipe for double stuffed pigs in a blanket, or sword fight, as he liked to call them, but on this side, what he had first seen as pretty paper, instead was something else entirely.

"How can—" Tim started.

"Because I can read Elvish, Tim," Shafty said slowly and then paused before continuing: "Tim, this is a spell of forbidden elven magic... from the first empire."

Tim peed a mild amount onto the floor.

He closed his eyes and decided not to read any of the words on the page. That sounded smart.

"Forbidden like... it wasn't any good, so they just decided to forget about it?" Tim asked, praying to the gods for just once to be right.

"No, like it was hidden because it very nearly destroyed the world during the first war against Elves and Dwarves," replied the weapon.

Tim peed some more.

"Have some backbone, Tim," Julie said, looking annoyed at the growing puddle on the floor.

"SHUT UP, JULIE, SHUT UP NOW. Do you have any idea what you have done?" Tim shrieked.

"Not getting my deposit back for this rental, that's for sure," Julie muttered.

"NO, YOU FUCKING FAT IDIOT. You sold untold forbidden magic to anyone that asked you for it. My gods, we thought it was for recipes. What would slavers and necromancers want with cake?" Tim leered at Julie.

"Everyone eats, Tim," Julie said, looking a bit more nervous.

At last, Tim looked down at the page. Boy, was that a mistake.

"Tim, wait," Shafty started, but it was already too late.

As soon as Tim opened his eyes, a golden beam of light shot up from the page and entered his face in the dreaded triad. His eyes, nose, and mouth were enveloped by the light that somehow had physical substance; all Tim could do was scream.

23

Sometime later, Tim woke up soaking in his own piss puddle on the floor. Julie and Tink were sitting on one of the comfortable-looking couches, and each had a hand on Shafty. Tim could see them laughing. Tim sat up and tried to speak through the overwhelming amount of drool that had somehow left his mouth.

Tim tightened his fist.

"I hate today so much," he said quietly in a very defeated tone.

"Ey, Tim! I was just telling the boys about that little snack I gave you the other day," Tink said laughing.

"Poop," Julie said.

"We don't have time for this," said Tim, coming over and sitting on the couch next to them.

"Tink, did the 'boys' get you caught up on what's happened?"

"What do you think we've been laughing at, Tim? You are such a terrible wizard. You are fat, you are lazy, considerably dumb, haven't mastered a minor floating spell that would've saved you from all of this, and then, to top it off, you have been ruining one of the most powerful magical artifacts in the world with your recipes, and... and..." Tink started laughing again, then continued, "your assistant has some sort of sick sex crush on you to the tune of selling the most dangerous magic in the world to any and all scum that asked!"

Tim just nodded as he was trying to understand all the symbols and words that had been tossed into his head when the light facefucked him... or whatever had happened.

"What was that?" Tim thought to Shafty.

"I gave you the ability to read elven runes," the spear said.

"Why?" he asked.

"Honestly, at this point, I don't think you can make it any worse. Maybe we can use the magic to undo what you've done," the magical spear replied.

"Maybe I should give it a test drive," said Tim to himself.

Julie nodded his agreement with a finger stuck deeply up one nostril. Tink nodded too, and Shafty gave his consent via telepathy. The unlikely party left the home that Julie definitely wasn't getting his security deposit back for and walked out into the street. They had overworn their welcome, and all four of them just wanted to get out of this dog-smelling pit of a town. But first, a bit of the ole razzle dazzle: magic.

Tim surveyed the hole these dog men called a town below him

like the axe of an angry god ready to drop on an unsuspecting tree stump. At this point, he noticed a nice abutment sticking out over the "city" — city in quotes because Tim was pretty sure he had taken dumps in fields that had more structure than this place. Walking out along the stone, Tim looked down and saw he had somehow still stepped in dog shit, unbelievable. Tim cleared his mind and focused on where he was walking; he liked how it pointed straight as an arrow at the dreaded arena — the prison that had taken so much girth from him. It would be his test batch. He was going to ask Shafty how to access his new arcane knowledge when he just opened the book and decided to read the first spell that he came to, Conflagration.

Without even thinking, Tim's hands began to move as fast as they did going down a buffet line. The spell climaxed with Tim's hands shooting outward as hot ropes of thick flame erupted from everywhere. Tim was impressed at the size of his magical comeuppance. He supposed it was so impressive due to the fact that his magical energy hadn't had a proper release since he arrived here. Tim felt dirty afterwards.

He walked away, assuming the magic would run its course. He approached his fellows and noticed they were all still watching the aftermath of the spell, their mouths agape.

Tim turned around and his malaise morphed into horror as he saw the size and extent to which his seed had grown. It was the largest fire he had ever seen, and it was showing no end in sight.

"Maybe we should get out of here?" Tink asked.

"Yeah, let's fucking go," Tim agreed.

*T*he party made their way to the outskirts of town, Tink leading the group and Julie gargling out directions as best as he could. With each step, the flames grew hotter and larger, and the barking of the hounds grew louder. Their target was a small, not often used stable near the entrance to one of the large tunnels that led off to the depths of the Down Under.

They all crouched behind a boulder and looked over at the stable. Tim was surprised to see that it had a man-made build to it, possibly even Myrmidian architecture by the look of it. He quickly ducked, however, when a band of goblins rode out of the stable with their giant pig mounts, snarling at the still-growing flames behind.

"Holy popover, that's a lot of bacon!" Tim hissed.

Julie and Tink had both been too short to see over the stone, and each was trying to stand and hop on their tiptoes to see over the lip of the ledge.

"Stop it, you fools," Tim rebuked.

Tink harrumphed,

"I kill monsters, wizard. I just wanted to have a little look…"

Tink attempted to poke his head around the corner of the stone and was promptly thwacked by Tim's sweaty palm.

"Wait just a minute."

Tim lifted his slightly bulbous head over the lip and saw that the coast was clear. He made a scurrying motion with his hands that Tink did not appreciate, and the trio made their way into the large wooden barn.

If Tim hadn't spent the last couple of months covered in every bodily fluid imaginable from a diverse host of creatures, the smell emanating from the kobold barn would have been the worst thing he had ever smelled. There was so much feces Tim couldn't even classify most of it, and not for the first time, he was thankful that Leslie wasn't here; the gods know they would have never gotten her to leave.

The little group began peering into the various closed and open stalls for a ride out of there. Tink was the first of the group to find what he was looking for.

"Hey!" Tink shouted,

"I got one!"

"What is it?" Tim asked as he and Julie dawdled over.

Tink was standing just inside a sealed-off door. Tim stepped in and immediately stepped back out again.

"What the fuck is that, Tink?" Tim asked nervously.

"It's a digger!" he said excitedly.

"What's a digger?" asked Tim.

"About the only thing those damn Dwarves do right," Tink responded.

Tink began to rummage through a pile of tack on the floor, picking out a saddle and bit for the monstrosity. Tim honestly had never seen a digger or anything like it before. He was pretty sure he had never even heard of one, but then again, Dwarves were not very well known in the realms of men. Really only the great trading caravans have any contact. From what Tim could see, this was a giant bear-looking creature who was a good bit bigger than a horse and had the largest claws Tim had ever seen.

"Is it for fighting? Looks like the meanest bear I've ever seen," Tim said.

"No, you daft chungus, the diggers are for digging. See those claws? They dig tunnels nearly big enough for you to waddle through. I don't know about your oversized blueberry of an assistant though," Tink said with a laugh.

Tim crept back nervously, still not trusting the great clawed beast. Speaking of giant blueberries, where had Julie gotten off to?

"Good kitty. Pretty kitty. Sweet kitty," was what Tim heard coming from the cracked door a few down from the monstrous sloth beast.

Julie giggles,

"No, no, kitty. Don't kiss my toes!"

"What the fuck?" Tim said as he walked into the room

that Julie was in.

As soon as he stepped into the room, the first thing that Tim noticed was that the animal Julie was giggling with was, in fact, not a cat. It was the largest wolf—or at least an approximation of a wolf—Tim had ever seen. It was definitely of wolf stock but stood about six feet at the shoulder and had muscle proportions that were all wrong. It was much more muscular than any wolf Tim had ever seen. Wolves, like other natural predators, had a lean hardness to them, something Tim didn't ever want to personally experience. This thing had the look of a wolf that was bred to be muscled and mean. If he had had any piss left in him, he would've let it go.

As soon as the giant dog saw Tim, it let out a low guttural growl that told every fiber in Tim's being to run. Julie was rolling around on the floor in front of it like the mentally deranged creature he was, and as the beast growled, he reached up into its mouth and said,

"No, kitty."

To Tim's utter shock, the dog stopped, lay back on the ground, and began playing with Julie.

"This is such a weird place," muttered Tim to himself.

Tim hated to admit it, but he was quite jealous. Tink and Julie had both found something awesome to ride, and so far, he hadn't found bunk. Each room he checked was empty and ransacked like everyone had left in a hurry. Which he guessed they had, and he knew that was slightly more than his fault. Tim looked down at the recipe book still in his hand; he really needed to get a lock for this thing.

As Tim contemplated simply burning the book or hiding it in the stable and just forgetting about it, Shafty spoke up.

"Tim, it's time to move. There are a bunch of angry

kobolds coming up from the town. Check the last stall."

Tim still thought Shafty was acting a bit strange. Ever since meeting Julie, and then the whole magic face-fuck incident, the weapon had been pretty quiet. But as he thought of this, he began to hear the sounds of approaching kobolds.

"Tim!" Tink shouted. "We've got to go!"

And Tim saw that the other two were taking their mounts out of the stable. Tim ran to the last stall and opened the door and standing in a large pile of hay was a rather chunky donkey.

"Oh, for fucks sake," Tim said, looking desperately around the rest of the barn and checking a couple of other half-opened doors, hoping against hope that on the other side would be a phoenix or some sort of intelligent tiger that wanted to be his friend but… there was nothing.

Jogging back to the "chonkey," Tim looked around. The beast was already saddled at least, so that would save him some time. On the wall, he saw a small copper name plate etched with the name "Pig" on it.

"Pig?" Tim asked.

The donkey stopped eating and gave him a sidelong quizzical glance. Tim thought that might be a yes.

"Pig," he said again with a bit more confidence, and not knowing exactly how to call a donkey, he made a padding gesture on his piss-soaked knees. To his surprise, the donkey stopped what it was doing and trotted over to Tim. Pig was waving its tail, which he thought was a good sign.

The next thing that happened Tim took as less of a good sign. Pig stood up on its hind legs and put his front legs on Tim's shoulders. It then made a loud hee-hawing *moo* sound and began nipping at Tim's neck. Tim hated this immensely.

In his haste to escape, Tim found himself turned around with the donkey behind him. This turned out to be a less than desirable position as now the donkey began to thrust wildly and seemingly to some sort of rhythm. Tim eventually broke away from the Julie of donkeys and tried to indicate to Pig that he just wanted to be friends. Pig was not getting the memo.

Eventually, Tim led the beast outside, which led to great shrills of laughter from Tink and Julie.

"Not a fucking word," Tim said as he tried to mount Pig, who was, in turn, trying to mount Tim.

"Just what you needed, Tim, another boyfriend," Tink said with a wink.

Tim heard Julie growl at this, but he really just didn't have the time. As he was playing sexual ring-around-the-rosy, the pack of angry dog men was approaching fast. At some point, it seemed even Pig got this message, and Tim was eventually allowed to crawl on top of the beast.

The three friends and their mounts, and a magical telepathic weapon, rode out together and headed for the nearest passage that led to anywhere else in the Down Under. Not ten minutes outside of town, they came to their first literal hurdle: a small, cobbled kobold bridge had broken under the weight of Tink's digger, with Tim and Julie on the wrong side of the bridge.

"Dammit, Tink. You had to pick the fattest, dumbest thing in that barn, didn't you?" Tim spat.

"Well, no, I believe the donkey made that choice," Tink answered.

"Ooh, burn," Julie said; even he knew that was a good one.

While Tim wondered what to do, Julie and Kitty simply leapt across the gap. It wasn't a very long bridge, and Julie's powerful mount took it in stride.

Not waiting for deliberation on the subject, Tim readied Pig and took a few donkey lengths back from the bridge. He then kicked Pig with all his worth and charged the donkey at the small wooden bridge. They were gaining speed and Tim was gaining confidence in their chances. A step away from the bridge, however, Pig slammed on the brakes, and Tim went tumbling off the donkey and onto the now shattered bridge.

Tim was falling… again.

*T*im sat about two feet under the bridge in a puddle of what above ground would be called industrial runoff; however, underground, it was more than likely animal waste. Pig tiptoed to the edge of the bridge and leapt over the narrow gap to join the group waiting on the other side. Tim hated himself and everyone else in the whole world.

Climbing up was an awkward affair for Tim. The bridge was just high enough that it was weird to pull himself up, and in every direction, the grips were just a bit too far. After a few minutes, he eventually scrambled his way up and found everyone having a rest without him.

"Thanks for the help, assholes," Tim said without any hint of cheer.

He looked at the assembled group and couldn't help thinking what a freak show this was. There was Julie, curled up with the most ferocious dog anyone had ever seen. Tink was examining the near-foot-long razor-sharp claws of his massive troglobitic sloth. And last, his own slack-jawed donkey was cozying up to the magical elven spear that Tim had just noticed was missing from his back.

"You know I am all for taking a break, but we are still so close to the town that the fire is making me sweat, and I can smell burning dog hair… maybe we walk for like a half hour?" Tim said, shaking his head.

"How am I the reasonable one?" Tim thought.

"We are all going to die," Shafty said telepathically.

"Oh, most definitely," replied Tim.

After quite a bit of cajoling, Tim convinced the others to get up and even managed to mount Pig without too much of a sexual back-and-forth. The group set off and put some ground between them and the possible war crime they had just committed to-gether.

Further along the trail, the group exited the kobold cavern and came to a large overlook set high above a giant Down Under valley. They all agreed to set up camp here for a while and have that rest they had been talking about earlier. They set up first, securing their mounts… and Julie, who asked to be tied up with his dog beast.

Tink and Tim set out to see what all they had with them and just how screwed they might be as far as surviving long enough to escape. They only had the weapons they had escaped with; however, Tink had grabbed a saddle bag that had been stashed with the rest of his mount's tack. They opened it up and, to their utter astonishment, actually found a few things that would be considered useful. There were half a dozen loaves of a hearty black dwarven bread, a water skin with what tasted like hon-eyed mead, and a roll of golden dwarven coins along with a broach shaped like a three-headed hammer.

"They must have killed this dwarf on the road recently," Tink said, putting the items back in the pack and strapping them back to his mount.

"Lucky for us," he finished.

Tim found a large backpack in Pig's tack as well. Opening it up, they found no items of use except for about two dozen apples.

As Tim examined one, he looked over at Pig, who had been staring at him for roughly the entire time they had been on rest but now looked even more predatory. Luckily for Tim, this staredown was broken by Julie, who rolled up on them, apparently done with his lying around with his new pet dog. For once, Julie seemed to be on the same page and pulled out a large pack that had been concealed under his cape.

"Julie always hungry," he said and dropped the pack on the ground.

To Tim's even greater surprise, the sack hit the dirt with a meaty *thump*.

"What in the..." Shafty thought.

"My thoughts too, Shafty," Tim replied.

Julie sat down by the pack, unbelted the straps, and pulled out a carefully wrapped package. Tink and Julie gathered around the slowest of their group.

"What is it, Julie?" Tim asked, his mouth already salivating.

Anything Julie would take so much care of had to be something truly delicious.

"Find a new recipe or two I did," Julie said, nodding enthusiastically.

Very gently, Julie unwrapped the bundle and revealed a small, sleeping furry creature.

"What the hell is that, Julie?" Tim asked, staring down at what he could only think of as an adorable, chubby-cheeked little bundle.

"Is that… is that… what I think it is, Julie?" Tink said, taking a step back.

In Tim's mind, Shafty began to yell,

"Quick, Tim, quick, you must kill it!"

"Wait, what?" Tim said aloud and in his mind simultaneously.

As he asked the question, the answer was gasped.

"Chinchilla!" Tink screeched with horror.

As Tink yelled, the little chinchilla sleepily yawned and opened one of his big, beautiful blue eyes. Tim could not figure out what the big deal was, and before he found out, he watched as Julie finished unwrapping the little fellow, held him to the group, and then promptly snapped its neck.

"Julie, what the fuck?!" Tim screamed and knocked the now lifeless chinchilla from Julie's sticky grasp.

"We're safe," Shafty said, and Tim could tell that Tink looked relieved as well.

"What the fuck is wrong with all of you? That was a fat baby squee-rrel and Julie just murdered it!" Tim said.

"Did you just say squirrel?" Tink asked. "That was no 'squee-rrel' you sugar-soaked oaf. It was the incarnation of evil itself, a baby chinchilladad."

"Isn't a chinchilla just a chunky squee-rrel? Do they get bigger than this?" Tim asked.

Tink slapped himself.

"Tim, I swear to the gods. I could not have picked a less worldly wizard than you. You don't know what a chinchilladad is?"

Tim grabbed the lifeless chinchilla corpse from the floor and held it up like,

"It's this? This is what you all are going on and on about, right? A fat squirrel beast."

"Sit down, Tim; you too, Julie. I think we are all in a lot more trouble than even I realized."

As they made a fire and sat down to some of the almost edible dwarven bread, Tink told Tim and Julie who and what the Chinchilladads were. Every subterranean race knew and feared them. They all avoided coming within a hundred miles of a chinchilla den. The Chinchilladads were subterranean fat-cheeked little monsters that, over the ages, had grown to roughly the size of a dwarf but quite a bit chonkier, which was only exacerbated by their thick coat of fine fur.

The earliest accounts of the Chinchilladads came from the food-loving and peaceful Guinea Pogsmen, who lived in the foothills of the southern mountainous jungle that separated the two great land masses of this part of the world. The Dwarves and many other races had once enjoyed steady trade with the Pogsmen. Their fine-tasting fruits and seeds were traded amongst all the civilized cities of Dwarves and Elves. Slowly, the flow of pog trade had been choked off, and their counterparts went to search them out to find out why.

What they found, instead of quaint farming villages, were gaping burned holes in the ground and the scattered corpses of very few pogs. Eventually, a dwarven party exploring the area around an old pog village found a deep tunnel that led them to the first city of the Chinchilladads.

What the dwarves found there was a horrible matrilineal society of necromantic high priestesses, who grew fat by literally eating the fresh meat of their own children. The males live pointless lives as breeders for the women or are neutered at birth and serve as a shock troop for the priestesses.

But the Pogsmen suffered a worse fate. They were forced into slavery to feed the masses of ever-growing chinchillas, and most of their children sacrificed to the darkest god of them all, the dreaded Cheeksasquattle.

Cheeksasquattle's thirst for the blood of baby pogs never lessens, and her horrible eye wanders to the children of men and dwarves. The first dwarven party escaped with their lives, but many more have not been so lucky. Each year, a bit of the Down Under is lost to the creeping monster, and every dwarven man shudders at the fate of those who have fallen. For the worst of it is, if you fall to a chinchilla, you will serve them ever after. In a twist of cruel fate, their necromantic god has granted them a spell to bind the dead to them, enslaving the deceased until absolute destruction of their corpses sets them free.

When the Chinchilladads come, it's after waves and waves of dead pogs and anyone else that has been unfortunate enough to pass their way.

"Holy fucking shit! Tink, are you serious?" Tim screamed and threw the dead baby chinchilla out of his sight. Julie moaned.

"Yes, Tim," Tink said, chewing on the dull end of a dagger.

"That wee bastard there is the most evil thing in these tunnels. If your monster, Julie, hadn't killed him, I would've done it myself."

"So, is there a country of these things? A kingdom? Who's their leader?" Tim asked.

Tink responded,

"Aye, they call it the Cheeks Empire, and yes, they do have a leader, the high priestess of Cheeksasquattle herself... Karen."

"Karen?" Tim said, tasting the word.

"Sounds a bit unassuming if you ask me."

"Unassuming?" Tink retorted.

"There isn't a more evil creature in this world! She eats a dozen freshly born babies every day. She single-handedly ordered and led the extermination of the Pogsmen and is hundreds of years old. She has killed more sentient creatures than anything living. Unassuming my gnomish ass, Tim."

"So, these little squee-rolls sound pretty bad then," Tim said.

Tink slapped himself and just nodded. Then, almost as a casual throwaway, Tim looked over at Julie.

"Julie, how many spells did you give to the... the... chinchillys?" Tim asked.

Julie held up all the fingers on his hands. Tim began to count out loud.

"1, 2, 3, 4, 5, 6, 7, 8... wait a second," Tim gasped.

"How many did you sell them, you fat fuck!?" Tink screeched, pulling his sword.

Tim broke the two miniature people up from their fight and said,

"Wait, wait, wait… Julie, you only have eight fingers?"

Julie nodded.

"Is that normal?"

"Julie always have these in this body," he replied, holding up his blood-stained fingers, and then he began to clean them with his giant lolling tongue.

The general sight of glee on Julie's face might have been the most disturbing part of Tim's day.

"Do the chinchillas make all that's happened worse?" Julie said.

Tink nodded in confirmation and said,

"We are proper fucked."

*T*he rest of the break went by without much talking, each of the companions letting the full weight of the day's events sink in and each dealing with it in his own way. Tink stayed busy with the weapons and tools at his disposal, Tim dreamed of overeating, and Julie, like always, sought out sex with something strange. Tim awoke to Julie's familiar screams.

"TIMMMM! MASTER!" the plump halfling screamed.

Tim snuffled loudly, and before he knew it, he found himself on his feet, jogging reluctantly over to Julie, who was still screaming his name. Then Tim slowed his trot; this whole active lifestyle was really starting to get to him, and he decided that if it was something that couldn't wait the few extra seconds it would take for him to arrive walking, then what could he really do about it in the first place?

Greeted by Julie and Tink's impatient stares, Tim arrived at the precipice the two tiny terrors were staring over and gesticulating wildly at. Tim, walking up to the edge cautiously, was pleased that he was breathing steadily and not winded anymore. Tim hated being tired more than anything else in the world, and if these two wanted his help, a wheezing, angry Tim would take much longer to reel in and get on topic.

Tim was just about to mention this point to the pair when he looked off the ledge and saw what they were pointing at.

Spread out in the under valley below their encampment was a mass wave of all the denizens that had dwelled in the town before Tim set it ablaze. There were dogs, some sort of bipedal cat-people, dark elves, dark dwarves, goblins, orcs, trolls, and a cadre of other enslaved and free monsters alike. Tim had never seen a parade of evil quite like that before him.

As Tim and his friends stood on the ledge overlooking the group, one of the dogs leading the pack began to sniff the air all around him and finally looked up towards the group.

"Hey! It's that asshole Tim!" one of the dogs barked.

"He took our jobs!" yelled another.

Then the entire wandering herd began to bellow in rage in their various roars and racial tongues. All with one demand: Tim's life.

Tim, as poetic as ever, just said,

"Oh fuck."

He even caught Tink slapping Julie on the back of the head as the little halfling echoed,

"Tim, Tim, Tim!"

The three adventurers didn't have time to chat about their feelings and come up with any plan other than to race to their various mounts and keep following the path up and out. Julie was the first to set off on his great canine mount, bounding off with its slack-jawed rider giggling the whole way. Tink and his digger were next, heading off in a decent trot behind the great dog, and lastly, Tim wrestled his way on top of his sexually frustrated chonkey and kicked his heels in. Pig did not move.

"Mush!" Tim bellowed and pointed dramatically at Tink's receding back.

"Woosh!" Tim tried flapping his arms down to his sides.

"Let's go!" Tim said, kicking in on the donkey again.

Shaking his head in puzzlement, Tim could not remember what he had done differently to get the donkey to go last time. Bringing his hand down, Tim lightly struck the rump of the large donkey, and to his surprise, that got it moving. After several minutes of trying, Tim learned that his new steed was essentially powered by slaps to the ass and that it was affected by frequency as well as strength.

He and Julie really should swap, Tim thought, as he slapped his hands furiously against the rump of his steed.

*T*he party of seven made their way up an ill-used path whose only markers were bits of goblin and kobold clothing attached to piles of rocks or the odd stick that must have been brought down specifically for the purpose. After several hours of steady climbing, the group lost the sounds of their pursuers and passed from the relatively empty lower caverns to one of the higher biomes in the great Down Under.

The area they had been in, and where the kobolds had lived, was a giant, nearly lifeless cavern with relatively smooth sides and ceilings along with pools of dark, cool water and a honey-comb of caves leading deeper down into the earth. This new biome was an under forest, according to Tink, and was very rare in the strata that Tink had always lived in, but apparently became more common the higher one climbed.

The group marveled at what they saw ahead. Instead of a glowing forest of fungus, an actual forest of trees lay spread out before them. The forest was also strange in the fact that it was all contained in one large circular cavern that seemed to stretch off as far as Tim could see, but there didn't seem to be nearly as many cracks or side passages as the areas below.

"What made the great circles, Tink? It almost doesn't look natural to me," Tim asked.

"Depends on what you consider natural. I've seen the bones of one of the beasts that used to dig these tunnels, a worm the size of… well the biggest thing I've ever seen. They ride through and eat the stone, leave their waste behind, and apparently, the soil is strong enough that regular plants grow in here."

As Tink described the process, Tim could see giant marks in the ceiling where the great beast's maw had torn the stone free and then ground it into the earth beneath his feet.

The plant life, though it was not fungal in nature, was certainly not normal. The trees displayed the same glowing features Tim had seen in those unfortunately shaped mushrooms, but their broad and thin leaves made them have a feel of the fantastic and the unknown. Tim wondered how many other wonders he had missed out on by sitting in a fart-smelling room with Julie. They saw bugs the likes of which they had never seen before. Julie couldn't count the number of new things to eat, or know which ones caused the tremendous pain in his guts, but he certainly intended to find out.

"One of my masters died in a place like this. These caverns often harbor other dangers than just the plant life," Shafty said and made what would pass as a coughing gesture, linking a small image of Julie to Tim.

Tim looked over and saw Julie rolling up one of the glowing leaves with a host of unknown bugs and other plant life on it, like a taco with actual mystery meat. Tim mentally shrugged to Shafty and thought,

"Worst thing that could happen is he will die."

"Will take more than that to kill a creature such as he," Shafty thought back.

Tim lifted up his crossed fingers and rode his faithless steed onward. The path of the ancient wyrm led up and up until, at last, the friends saw a glimmer of starlight. With the open air waiting for them and an army of displaced kobolds behind, they were all anxious to get back home.

28

Dick was riding hard and fast. If there was one thing he hated besides a quick in and out at a profitable trade spot, it was being rubbed raw on a fleeing wagon. He knew the badlands were a dangerous place, always had been.

Rival traders, goblins, centaurs, and the like never made a trade easy, but bringing a fully loaded wagon in and out of a dwarf trade post made silver fall like rain, and Slick Dick was a thirsty caravanner indeed.

This trade had been different from the get-go though; things was off, and nothing felt quite right to ol' Dick.

The caravan had turned about halfway up to the dwarven hold, they were too far out of the way to make for bargain town, and for the last two days, Dick had seen the loping ghosts of mounted goblin riders and their wolf mounts shadowing him and his friends.

Didn't smell right.

The next part of the trail was most likely going to be the point where they make it or break it. The rocks were getting close, and the bridge over the water was not an ideal spot. So, Dick decided he would rise to the occasion and held up his hand to give the signal for the wagons to circle. It was now or never.

The wagons of a trading caravan were not like the wagons of a farmer or a simple trader. A caravanner from the wild lands was a different beast entirely. They were usually more than a match for a single wandering band. Dick hopped up from his seat and pulled the copper lever by his side. As the lever was pulled, the long wagon out behind him began to bend and take shape, rattling and hissing as it went. He pressed two more buttons beside it, prompting pieces of metal to jut out from both ends and form into thin but sturdy metal walls that met up with neighboring wagons. In the span of just a few minutes, his wagon train of fifteen wagons became a circular fort of metal and thick wooden beams.

Dick hopped from the well-worn seat of his rattle wagon and began to shake the dust from his goblin skin chaps.

"Was time for a stretch anyway," Dick said to himself as he continued to shake out the dust.

Dick was long and lean, his hair was the color of the sun, and his eyes were green, which stood in stark contrast to the first driver to reach him.

"What the hell, Dick?" Coppereye Jake asked.

Coppereye was Dick's closest competition for rattle wagon leader and always came in just shy of Dick's sales numbers. Whereas Dick liked to deal in dwarven goods and spirits to men, as well as leaf to the dwarves, Coppereye sold a whole mess of magical concoctions to anyone they came across, with varying degrees of success. Sometimes, his goods were better than advertised, but more than once, he had been accused of the most dreaded of titles: snake oil salesman.

Where Dick was tall and thin, Coppereye was fairly short and
stout, but his stoutness was bred from pure muscle, and the
large hammer he wore strapped across his back was certainly
not just for show.

"Don't like the look of these rocks, Cop'," Dick said, pulling out his rapier and testing its edge on his finger.

Dick applied one of Copper's own concoctions down the length
of the blade and made careful work to not let it get on his skin.
Dick also checked the chambers on his pocket cross. A handy
little invention of Dick's own design. He sold it as a hand crossbow, but it used a different force to launch the projectiles. It was
a great way to start any party.

"Ah hell, slick. You said that when we turned around
two days ago. I ain't seen shit out here 'cept for a herd of cents',
and they didn't even looked at us twice," said Coppereye.

"Maybe," Dick said and gave his sword a few practice
thrusts.

Centaurs were either a whole heap of trouble or were good for
a buck. These had been… restless. Which made Dick ever more
nervous.

The next wagoner to approach the group was Necromancy Jane.
An odd choice for a wagoner, Jane dabbled in the necro as a kid,
and instead of running off to join an evil army or something
similar, she started going around and bringing back peoples'
dead. Sometimes it's just for a short talk, sometimes it's to ask
where they put their favorite pipe, and one time, it was for a
wife to beat her husband back to death. She sure didn't make
anything boring. Wasn't bad to look at either, Dick thought, and
not for the first time. Yep, one of these days, he was going to ask
her over for supper.

"Got a bad feelin', Dick?" Jane asked as she tried to fan herself from the heat.

She subconsciously began to check the dagger on her belt and flexed her fine little fingers. Dick suspected they were capable of more than one kind of magic. As Dick started to reply, a flurry of arrows rained down and each one that struck a wagon made a hard *thunk* as it stuck deeply into the hardwood.

"I told you I had one!" Dick screamed at Copper and Jane.

"Might not matter either way, Dick!" Copper screamed as the large swarm of goblins and their wolven mounts began to circle the fortified wagons.

"What do you think, Jane?" Dick asked, as he reached up to the side of his wagon and pulled out his heavy crossbow.

This baby was for range; anything it stuck, only needed it once. Jane didn't answer. Her eyes were open, but they had already turned bright green. They always did that when she began to channel the dead. Dick slowly lifted his head above the wagon and tried to make a quick account of what he saw.

"Looks to be nearly fifty riders and maybe another ten or so taking shots from the ridge…"

That wasn't great news. A band usually wasn't any more than a dozen raiders trying to make a quick getaway. Fifty was something else entirely. Dick's crossbow twanged.

"Make that nine," he finished with a smile.

Either way, Dick was going to take a whole heap of them with him.

"Sixty is twice too many, Dick!" Copper yelled and began to comb through his jacket, looking for a particular scroll.

"We've fared worse," replied Dick.

"Yeah, and we lost twenty wagons!" Copper shot back.

Jake wasn't wrong; their caravan still hadn't recovered from their last run-in with Chicken Bone Grutz. Dick considered him his personal nemesis, and in all of the great rolling hills and plains of the western borders, he had never met a gob that was worse than ol' Chicken Bone.

Finally finding the scroll he was looking for, Copper stood up and began to read the arcane words. As he finished, a gout of flame shot from the air and landed in the middle of several of the riders. Two died right then and there, and several others rode off howling and smoking. Dick nodded to Copper, and as he looked up, he saw Jane begin to wander out from the fortifications, her wagon's parcels unwrapping themselves.

The rest of the group were holding their own as well. A couple of the elves were standing on the tallest wagon, hitting everything they shot at. As Dick was about to turn, he saw one of them take a stone spear to the leg and topple off the wagon.

Cursing their luck, he turned back to Jane, who was just about to start her show. This was Dick's favorite bit. Jane would pick up various bodies from fights, as well as a few they procured along the trail, and would reanimate them for a little song and dance number. Though they were usually light on the singing…

A few human corpses were the first to crawl out, followed by a dozen goblins in various states of decay, but Jane's prized jewel was a mostly intact buffataur. Buffataurs are the great plains version of a Minotaur and are somewhere around twice the size. This particular buffataur was a several-ton male, and Jane now rode on his shoulders.

Jane and her undead posse tore into the next group of passing goblins, and Dick didn't want to miss out on the fun. Leaping over the wagons, Dick unsheathed his rapier and joined the fight. He was followed by another half dozen of the menfolk from the caravan, each wielding their preferred weapon of war. Caravanners were always ready for a fight.

Dick hated fighting goblins; they weren't very good at it. His rapier was meant for back-and-forth swordplay followed by equally cutting remarks. A more civilized form of combat. But instead, he found himself spinning here and diving into a heart there. It just wasn't as fun.

Dick looked up in time to see Jane get knocked off of her mount and tumble to the ground. As she hit the ground, her head must have struck a rock because she went limp, and so did all of her creations. Hell, even the goblins stopped. Dick didn't wait. He thrust his sword into one paused goblin's throat and ran over to Jane.

There was some blood on the back of her head, but it didn't seem too bad. As Dick looked up, he figured their trail was over as the circling goblins looked down at them with hungry eyes. Dick was just about to make his peace with the sweet embrace of death as he pulled out his hand bow but stopped when he heard a very strange sound.

"Fuck, fuck, fuck..." he heard someone cursing in the distance.

For the second time that day, the battle between the caravan and the goblins was halted as all raised their eyes to see what awful fucker was coming over the closest rise. To the surprise of everyone, the half-ass wizard, Tim, was riding his faithless steed, Pig, ass-backwards into a battle waged between men, goblins, and the largest undead creature Tim had ever seen.

From Tim's vantage, which was at present the ass end of a donkey, he saw a huddled man and woman that Pig leapt over, and then he began to see the crumpled forms of goblins being left in Pig's wake. Pig had a passion for goblin killing in her blood, and that's a tale Tim will one day find out for himself.

For now, Tim decided to shoot off a fireball using Shafty as a focus and shouted,

"OATMEAL CREAM PIE!"

Working with Shafty for the last few days as they made the great climb up from the Down Under had sharpened Tim's magical abilities somewhat, and to his delight, from Shafty's tip, shot a bowl-sized ball of fire. It struck a centered mass of mounted goblins and sent bits and pieces of them flying everywhere. As a finish, Shafty flew from Tim's hands and began to make its way through as many goblins as possible.

Dick's surprise was even more complete when a deformed, hairy baby-like creature leapt into the scrap riding a monstrous dog. Followed by what looked like a deep gnome riding a clawed monster. He watched in awe as they both began to rip apart the goblins.

Dick didn't know if he and his party were saved, or if he was just about to be eaten by the biggest ragtag bunch of creatures in existence. Deciding he didn't really want to wait and find out, Dick scooped up the still-unconscious Jane and bravely dashed across the narrow battlefield. After he dropped her off in the safety of the circled wagons, Dick gracefully leapt to the back of the battle-crazed donkey that was being ridden by the fat wizard.

"Howdy there!" Dick said, managing to tip his hat in a dramatic bow even though the two were in close quarters and on donkey back.

Now that Dick was close enough to hug the man, he wasn't entirely sure that he wanted to. The wizard, if that's what he was supposed to be, looked more like a wizard of the hobo variety. Being as far-traveled as he was, Dick knew a deviant when he saw one. The wizard's robes were filthy and appeared to be covered in as many different bodily fluids as it was in different patches of blood. The man himself was dirty and smelled like he had eaten a literal dick for breakfast, yet still had a sick sort of charm about him.

"They call me… Tim," the wizard said to Dick.

"Hey… I've heard that name somewhere—" Dick started and was stopped suddenly as he whipped out his rapier in a flourish and stuck its tip deep into a passing goblin.

The talk between the two stopped as Tim began to conjure up a few spells and Dick used his rapier to great effect. Between the two of them, the surging defenders of the wagon train, and Tim's very special partners, the group put the goblins on the run, and the cheers of men could be heard ringing throughout the small patch of rocks where they had made their stand.

The two eventually unmounted, and Dick led Tim and the donkey he had learned was named Pig over to the circular defensive structure. By applying a light kick to a hidden pressure plate, a large rod swung out, and Dick explained it was for tying up the animals. The three adventurers secured their steeds and walked in with Dick.

"What's the damage? How's Jane?" Dick asked as he jogged off towards one of the wagons.

"Lost one of the elven brothers, a couple other scrapes and bruises. One wagon was burned, but Jane is resting in her caboose," replied Coppereye.

Tim, Julie, and Tink all followed Dick towards the strange wagon he had entered. It was black and advertised quick meetings with the dead with bright purple and green letters on the side that read, "Necro Jane's Bone Gang." Tim didn't know if he should be confused or aroused; either way, he was both.

Looking around, they saw a host of other wagons, each offering different and exotic wares. The three were just circling about, unsure of where to go next, when Dick reappeared holding the arm of a bandaged woman.

"This is Jane," Dick said, continuing, "and if it wasn't for you fellas, I'm sure Jane and I both would be goblin food."

The three adventurers didn't really know what to say and just mumbled their acceptance and tried to bow to the lady.

"I would love to give you the copper piece tour, but I think we should move on a piece farther down the road first. The last trade post before we reach the inner kingdoms is about an hour over the bridge. It has walls, guards, and hot food that's not ours."

With that, Tim watched as the entire fortified camp fell away before him. Horses appeared from corrals, and before he knew it, the entire caravan was back in order and was slowly crossing the large stone bridge that spanned the huge rocky canyon below. Tim stayed on the wagon with Dick while Tink and Julie followed Jane back to her wagon. Tim didn't know what to make of the tall, laid-back trader at first, but after not long at all, he decided he liked him very much.

After about an hour on the trail, a large stone structure appeared, with high walls and guard towers at each of the corners. A general cry of "huzzah!" came up from all the tradesmen, and Tim found himself joining in. He hadn't been sure he was ever going to make it back to civilization again.

The caravan entered the fort and set up in its non-defensive configuration, which to Tim, was even more impressive than what it had been before. The fort they had entered was basically just what they had seen from the outside, four stout walls with large towers and one small structure off to the side that served as barracks for the garrison. The rest of it was a huge empty space where caravans set up. Tim watched in delight as each of the wagons turned into a store within itself, and from nothing, came a small frontier town.

"What magic!" Tim said to Dick.

"No magic here, Wizard. This is engineering. Come on, let me take you guys to dinner. I'm taking you to my favorite spot," Dick said, waving the monstrous trio over.

"This place is great. It's called the Bean 'n' Between," Dick continued.

"What's the bean in between?" Tim asked.

Dick turned a little red but answered,

"If you have to ask, you'll never know."

"Nerd," Shafty said condescendingly in Tim's mind.

"What? I don't get it," Tim muttered to himself in a frustrated tone.

Dick decided he needed a drink, and quickly. Luckily for everyone involved, a slightly healed Jane came in and took the center of attention from the strange, gathered group of males. The group began to exchange stories of the road. As Dick told of the disastrous calamities happening out on the great plains—the horrible firestorms and freak waves of water seemingly being let loose by random bandits and the like—a cold chill began to run up Tim's spine.

"It's all your fault, you know," Shafty communicated mentally to Tim.

"I know," Tim thought back.

Dick's caravan slowly fled from trade post to trade post, leaving the trade-sponsored forts behind and heading for what they thought would be the safety of the Myrmidian forts ahead. Along with Dick's usuals, they had added Tim and his misfits and whatever guards decided not to stick around for the enemy's torches… all the while picking up news of the new calamities ravaging the world. Each fort behind them was turned to ash as the growing horde of kobolds and goblins combined to pursue their shared tormentor, growing in strength as other denizens who also hated Tim decided to join.

On a soft, fog-filled morning, Dick's rattle wagon came to a seaside path high above the crashing waves, and they could finally see it: Myrmidon.

Myrmidon is the oldest and most powerful of the human kingdoms that dot the eastern shores of the great ocean. It also is the most southern and enjoys a milder winter along with a punishing summertime heat. The great city can be seen from sea or shore miles away, as its massive white walls glimmer in the ebb and flow of the sun's daily heat. It was the first human kingdom founded on the continent after the great battle fought at the Khan's Tooth.

"My gods, is everyone as moist as I am?" Tim said while trying to air out all his damp-prone locations.

He gave a quick slap to Julie as he found the little miscreant's hand also checking his taint area.

"No!" Tim shouted, his strike ringing on Julie's nose.

Julie mumbled something unintelligible and walked off, rubbing his face. He didn't understand this new adventuring Tim. He gave all the same signals, but every time he reached out for a snack, Tim punished him instead. His world was in such strange chaos. At least the "kitty" usually consented, Julie thought, as he went off to find his mount.

Dick had watched this whole bizarre affair and wondered, not for the first time, what in the fuck was going on between those two?

"Body men… what can ya do?" Tim said with a shrug and gave Dick a punch on the shoulder.

The two rode in silence for a few minutes while Dick desperately wondered just who and what he had brought to his favorite town to booze and schmooze in. Luckily for both, any further attempts at small talk were ended when a patrol of cavalry approached the haggard caravan. The captain of the patrol was well known to Dick, and he called out in greeting,

"Julius, what news from the city?"

"Dick, we haven't even straightened up your cell from the last time you were in town. Oh bother, I suppose a dirty one will have to do. Though, I am surprised to see you! Last we had word, the talk was Chicken Bone had finally gotten the better of you!"

The two grasped hands as Dick stepped off the rattle wagon.

"You should know better than to listen to rumors, Julius; I don't think I will be hearing from him for quite some time," said Dick.

"Trouble on the road?" Julius asked, giving Tim a less than approving glance. Dick looked at Tim as well.

"Yes, new friends. That wizard there, Tim is his name, saved Jan—"

"The Wizard Tim?" Julius interrupted, leaping from his horse. "Are you The Wizard Tim? The town wizard of Halfass?" The guard captain asked, approaching the still-seated Tim.

"I uh… hmmm… yes?" Tim finally managed to squeak.

"Good God, man! The entire city mourns your death, even on this very day." Looking over Tim's shoulder, something else caught Julius's eye as well. "And your little man, Julie?" Julius asked, pointing at a now perplexed Julie, who was hiding something behind his back.

"The mystery continues to deepen," Dick mumbled, confused at all the fuss.

"All of you with me," Julius said. "We will give you a hero's welcome into the city. All of Myrmidon will be open to you, my friends. You slick one, you," he said as he walked up and punched Dick entirely too hard in the arm.

"What the fuck is going on?" Dick said while rubbing his bruising arm.

"These two saved the kingdoms!" Julius said while mounting his horse.

"Trumpets!" he bellowed, pointing at two of his men. "You ride ahead. Open the gates! Make the announcement. Tim is here!"

As Julius and his men set off and the caravan fell in behind, Dick looked over at Tim and said,

"What kind of oil are you selling, Tim?"

Tim looked like he honestly did not know, and the truth was he had no idea what was going on. As the rattle wagons appeared at the gate, throngs of people rushed out into the streets and began cheering,

"Tim! Tim! Tim!"

Tim, not wanting to upset anyone, decided it was probably best to embrace this newfound fame just in case it came with some perks. If he was held in high enough esteem, he could maybe consider bringing up the displaced kobold army making its way towards the city and, of course, all the missing magic spells. But for now…

"Tim, Tim…" he said, cheering along with the crowd and doing the fancy hand wave he learned from the Halfass pumpkin queen.

He even held Julie aloft for a while. It made Julie feel like a young boy again, though he had technically never been young or a boy. The group followed and cheered down the entire main thoroughfare of the great city and led directly to the shining white walls of the seaside fortress. Tim had never seen the sturdy seaside keep before, but the stories of the great battles fought and won on its walls were legendary.

After the battle of Goblin's Head, the kingdom of Myrmidon was founded, and its ancient sons and daughters spread out to form all the other human nations. Tim could see the gold top gleaming from the sea serpent's tower. A lone green min-aret shining against a forest of white towers. It was the seat of magical power in the kingdom, and many argued that the most powerful magical user in the land dwelled within, the mighty wizard, Marlin.

"Tim, Tim, Tim!"

The crowd continued to chant as the caravan made its way through the golden gates and into the courtyard of the great cas-tle itself. The throngs of onlookers stopped at the gates, fearing the bolts of the many crossbows pointed their way, but were just as happy to keep yelling from the open street.

The Green Guard appeared to be a company of one hundred of Myrmidon's most elite knights, that traditionally perform guard duties and special missions for the royal household. This day, they were serving as an honor guard as the great Queen of Myr-midon herself stepped out onto the sun-brightened courtyard.

She pulled a slender white wand from, well, nowhere Tim could deduce, but that did not stop his imagination. She was a beauti-ful woman, and something about her struck at his memory…

"My people, my people," the queen said, the wand am-plifying her voice many times over.

A hush came over the gathered crowd at the request of their great queen.

"Our greatest hero, Tim, has returned, along with his… hmm… brave and very unique friends."

The queen continued to look over the motley group of monsters, trying not to make any sort of eye contact, then settled on star-ing contently at the unwashed masses gathered before her. They were like a soothing balm for her eyes.

"My daughter's savior has been returned to us from

the grave; we thank the great caravanners once again for their brave work. What kind of queen would I be without throwing a feast?"

The crowd cheered. Hushing them once again, she continued,

"This day and the morrow will forever be Tim's days! Let there be no work and much rejoicing for our great fortune!"

The crowd went wild.

Tim was trying to process any part of the information he was hearing when the crowd began to cheer even louder as two green knights escorted a familiar white-clad form from the castle to stand next to her mother. It was Aurora.

Tim's wand immediately went from its preferred button mode to extend. Julie, of course, noticed this.

"Aurora?" Tim squeaked.

"Tim!" she yelled and ran up to him but stopped short due to the nature of Tim's cloak and robe, which looked like those of a nefarious hobo who had exclusively used his clothes as a collection point for bodily fluids — both his own and others. Her quick run up to him ended anticlimactically as she gingerly patted his shoulder and then quietly cast a cleansing spell on her hands to wipe away the viscous fluid on her fingers.

Tim, with his continued lack of social skills, crowded closer in on her still and asked, "You're a princess?"

A short time later, Tim found himself in an absolutely luxurious bedroom, being fitted for some new clothes. Julie was there swinging his feet off the side of the bed, looking rather glum.

"I can't believe she hid it from us, Julie. A princess! Who would have ever guessed? It's so much better than just being rich. It's institutional wealth," Tim said.

Julie humphed as the seamstress measured Tim's inseam. As the seamstress finished her bizarre measurements, she felt less sure about exactly who, or what, was under that bedsheet. She had immediately thrown out the clothes he had been wearing. She had seen better rags lying beside a cheap whore's bed than what that beast had been wearing.

"Alright… err… guests of the majesties, I'll have you and your little wee thing something nice to wear for supper," the seamstress said.

As the hunched old thing shut the door behind her, Tim pulled his sheet up over his breasts and began to pace around the room. Tim had several things running through his mind: the marauding army, the missing spells, Aurora. But most of all, he was more than a little confused as to why everyone thought he was a hero. The worst thing he could do was say too much and spoil it.

With this new idea firmly in his mind, Tim was surprised to hear a sharp knock on the bedroom door. Nodding to Julie, the angry little miscreant hopped off the bed and went to answer the door. Without any pomp and circumstance, Julie walked over, slammed open the door, and then marched back over to the bed to continue his pouting. Tim observed this behavior and thought it most unbecoming for a body man, especially now that they were in high society. Looking at the stone doorway, Tim was surprised to see Sir Eric, Captain of the Green Guard and the very man who set Tim off on this adventure.

"Sir Eric!" Tim said and walked over, giving him a too warm hug.

"Ugh," Sir Eric grimaced as he pushed the sweaty wizard off his fine clothes. "Yes, Tim. Grand to see you, my friend."

Tim let his hand linger on Sir Eric's arm.

"I have come to collect you for a meeting. We have much to discuss. Close up your sheet and let us be off. "

Sir Eric walked quickly down the hallway, occasionally looking back at the bedsheet-clad wizard. Tim, was more often than not looking back behind him at the morose halfling who was following him, cursing the entire time and stopping to kick everything expensive and decorative along their path.

The trio arrived at a grand-looking set of thick wooden doors, which at their approach, opened to reveal an elegant marble chamber that overlooked the city far below. Inside, Tim could see nobles, wizards, and even a few friends. Tim saw Ayers, Leslie, Aurora of course, Dick, and to his surprise, sitting at the head of the table was Marlin. The most famous of wizards. The two had never met, but Tim was impressed with his regal bearing.

None of them even seemed slightly surprised to see Tim walk into the room with a bedsheet covering his bulky body. Sir Eric pointed out a large stool in the middle of the circular room for Tim and took Julie over to a small stool on the side where Tim noticed Tink was sitting.

As Tim sat down and began arranging the bedsheet around himself, Marlin the wizard struck his staff to the marble floor, and a loud ringing sound filled the room.

"Quiet down, quiet down, everyone. As we all know, this tower and kingdom have been filled with the tales and exploits of this unlikely hero sitting here before us. The Wizard Tim, is it not?" said the regal wizard.

"I... I... I... be... he..." Tim eventually spat out.

"We've been told of your exploits in the old dwarven town," Marlin said, "of your fearless charge on the bridge, and the great fireball that sent the hordes of goblins back to the deep. "

Murmurs and nods were seen around the room.

"What none of us have heard, however, is how you've come back to us and how your story, if at all, relates to the many abnormal events that seem to be happening around the world."

Tim sat very still, almost frozen.

"Can you enlighten us?" the old wizard asked.

"Well... I definitely cannot say for certain, Sir Wizard

and other important people. I have been a mere victim of circumstance whose bravery and strength helped me come out on top in most of these situations. I don't deserve your pity, just your eternal thanks, and perhaps a monetary award of significant value."

"Why, I nev—" The wizard started, but before he could continue, the large marble doors opposite him were pushed open, and in walked the queen.

"Marlin," the queen said loudly and firmly.

Everyone in the room stood upon her entrance, even Tim. Though his standing was accompanied by a loud ripping sound, and he could only wonder what part of him was exposed now; he could feel a slight breeze.

"Your Majesty," answered the bowed Marlin.

"I see that our hero has not even been allowed to be properly dressed before being dressed down by the once great and powerful Marlin. Did I not specifically command that Tim was to be left alone until after tonight's feast. Then, if at all, we would gather his statement and see if there was anything of value to add?"

"Well, I—" Marlin began.

"According to Aurora, the poor man is half-starved," the queen said, pointing at the still-not-skinny wizard who was just trying to make sure nothing popped out of his hands in the queen's presence. As many of you know, when working with certain-sized staffs, lighting and circumstance are very important for a reveal. This was not the place.

"I'm very sorry, Your Majesty," the wizard said, bowing again.

"We will pick this up tomorrow, everyone."

The crowd quickly dissipated, all trying to avoid the queen's gaze as they left the room. Aurora went to her mother and gave Tim a shy smile and a wave as she left. Tim spent the rest of the afternoon being tied and beaten down in a way he'd never consented to before as a team of women worked together to dress him in the quickly prepared robes they had brought to his chamber. He took the opportunity to reminisce about past group experiences, only to have his daydreaming cut short: one of them had commented on the large size of the bust, but when it fit Tim like two lopsided gloves, not another word was said.

Julie was dressed smartly in a suit befitting of a small flying ape, and the two looked the most presentable that perhaps they had ever been.

The feast was a grand affair with more food than Tim had ever seen in one place. Julie's pockets were full of new secrets, both taken freely and against others' wills. Tim was introduced to dignitaries, wizards, exotic animal dealers, and even the owner of the most famous pie dishery in all of the kingdom. How he wanted his life to be like this every day.

As the night wound down, Tim found himself on a balcony overlooking the peaceful city below. Behind him, he heard a stirring and saw a most welcome sight. His team of vagabonds, rogues, and even a princess had all found their way outside.

"Aye, laddie, we are all quite proud of ye. Even the great green monster over here cried when she thought ya went splat," Ayers said, punching Leslie on the shoulder.

"That's not true," Leslie barked drunkenly. "Julie seems to know his way around a latrine; I thought I would lose out on many future snacks!"

The whole group laughed awkwardly at how scared they were of Leslie and her disgusting habits. She and Julie were indeed quite the pair. Aurora came up and touched Tim's still-clean shoulder.

"Tell us what happened to you, Tim. Where did you go when you fell?"

Tim had his load on, so he decided, what the hell? Why not regale them with a doctored version of events?

Tim started with his and Julie's fall but decided to leave out the part about how Julie had likely caused it in the first place due to him having some sort of jealousy towards Leslie. Also, he omitted the part about how Eliza might have specifically targeted him due to their shared history and how that may or may not have led to her eventual capture and multiple assaults from orcs and their kind.

Instead, he painted it more as a lecture about the virtues of good and how, in an act of bravery, he blew up the bridge with no account for his own safety. He then told them of the magical and hallucinogenic dick forest and how that led to his servitude and gladiatorial feats under the watchful eyes of the kobolds that dwelled in the underground city.

He told them of Tink's bravery and his heritage of hunting monsters in the deep end of the Down Under. He recounted their escape and his harrowing tale of sexual assault and how it still made him cry at night. He told them about the tunnels and of the great skeleton wyrm that once made them. He then went on to tell of Dick and Jane's caravan and the marvelous inventions that are being traded out on the wild and open plains.

During all this, he also neglected to mention the fire that displaced the now roving army of kobolds. As well as his and Julie's involvement with the ancient spells and their subsequent release by agents of the darkest creatures in their world.

It was a good story, and some of it was even true.

The group of companions felt like they were on top of the world, with nowhere to go but up.

Weeks and miles away from Tim, a lone traveler braved the dark paths of the Down Under and found her way to the city of the great full-cheeked one, Cheeksasquattle. The city of the evil Chinchilladads was not a place one came and went, for its guards and workers were all undead.

Eliza saw huge numbers of the once thriving Guinea Pogs in various states of decay, tending to the menial work that kept the great black stone city functioning. At its center were the dark mountains of stone where countless thousands had perished in the name of the ever-hungry god. It was there, to the top of the central pyramid, that Eliza went. She climbed its blood-stained steps, kicking clumps of bloodied hair from her nice leather boots along the way.

The colossal center pyramid was a city in itself, serving one purpose and one master, the most evil necromancer of all the puffy-cheeked monsters, Karen.

Eliza would be the first to describe herself as a cold murderous bitch with designs of world domination and the destruction of the so-called "good" races, but next to Karen, she felt like a mere child. As she entered the sanctum of sanctums and looked upon the diabetic mass that served as the ruler incarnate of the Chinchilla race, she shuddered in fear.

Karen was a giant, even for the overfed priest rank of the Chinchilladads. Before her, lay a moving belt of plates, each with a live and kicking chinchilla child upon it. Each plate passed before Karen and was emptied down her huge, stinking gullet. With each sacrifice, a green flame of eldritch energy lit the thing's eyes, and Eliza knew that somewhere, an undead being was awakening, another soldier for the wars to come.

"Liza, my favorite hooooman, have you come to taste the delicacy of my children?" the necromancer asked with a bone-rattling cackle. Even for Eliza, the offer was revolting.

"No, great and powerful Karen. I have brought you something else."

Reaching into her bag, Eliza pulled out the choice bit of spells she had taken from that idiot janitor of Tim's and presented the pages to Karen.

"Delicious, delicious," the giant chinchilla howled.

Eliza leaned over her and flipped one of the pages over to reveal the spell hidden on the other side.

"By he whose cheeks were never empty, this is the most useful piece of paper I have ever seen," she hissed. "A delicious recipe for an apple turnover on one side and a spell to call forth a space creature on the other."

Karen pawed her full and bloodied cheeks.

"This Tim could be most useful to me."

"Tim is a fool. Let me end him and his little friends. Then your buffet of evil can truly begin!" barked Eliza.

Karen sat for a moment and thumbed through the list of spells, though Eliza could tell she seemed to spend more time on the recipes. Finally, she said,

"This one," and handed Eliza over a very nasty summons. "Take this and a squad of my undead minions. Let the above worlders know that their time runs short. The day of the weak-cheeked nears its end!"

—

For weeks, Eliza clawed through earth and stone, down emptied tunnels and winding rivers, before finally finding herself on the way to Myrmidon. As she did, she found that many of the outposts were already burned. When she was but a day or two out from that doomed city, she found out why.

Before her, lay the entire city of the great kobold underground, along with most of the other denizens that dwelled there.

Eliza cackled. This could not be going any better.

—

Tim looked out over the sea and took a deep, salty breath. He would have to get used to it if he finally seduced Aurora and became a prince. But he thought he could deal with it. He was trying to think of a way to make everyone leave when Sir Eric appeared at the door.

"Princess, gather your companions and your tools for battle. It seems some kobolds are attacking the city!"

"Fuck," said Tim.

"Fuck, fuck, fuck, fuck," Tim kept saying over and over again as he and his friends were ushered by Sir Eric, who was clad in his sea green battle plate.

Tim had already thought about trying to take off and find somewhere good to hide, but the green knights surrounded his party and ushered them from room to room. The group was taken to Marlin's tower, where he and the queen were overseeing the defense of the city.

"They've already overrun the lower quarters gates. They are pouring into the city," Marlin said to a very shaken queen at his side.

"How did this happen, Marlin? How did so many appear at our doorstep?" the queen asked.

The old wizard shook his head but gave Tim a long look.

"Tim, perhaps you… who just spent some time in a

kobold city, could tell us where all of these kobolds came from?" Marlin asked accusingly.

Tim looked around.

"I don't see how that's relevant," Tim replied rather flippantly.

Tim also would like to know how the old wizard bastard knew that. He had only told his friends who had been with him the whole time. He must have been spying on him. It was just so rude.

"Yes, a great idea, Marlin," the queen beamed.

"Tim, go out with my knights and see what you and my daughter's friends can reconnoiter about the invading force," the queen said and went back to looking at the table.

A most excellent idea, Tim thought... to escape.

Just a few short months ago, if you had told Tim that he would be rushing out of the castle of Myrmidon at the head of an elite squad of knights with his adventuring companions at his side, he would have asked you who you were and just how much of his diary you had read... and told you that those sketches were for research only. Yet here he was, racing out on his unfaithful donkey, Pig, into a city being overrun by an enemy army he had accidentally displaced with an ancient fireball spell that had wiped out their entire town and killed countless thousands. The real pickle, however, was how was he going to get out of this one. Everyone was riding so close to him that he could not very well ride off on his own.

"Alright, gather around everyone," he said to the crowd of knights and companions. "We need to split up into groups and... hmm... check all the gates... yeah... to see if any of them are still open. So... the people... yes, the people, can be escorted to safety."

Everyone looked around and nodded that the idea was a good one. Tim had just successfully lied and thought of an escape plan out loud, and it had worked. Genius.

"How many gates are there, Sir Eric?" Tim asked.

"Six, Tim," Eric answered.

"You better check the larger gates with the Green Guard. If those have been overrun, who knows what could be running amok there," said Tim.

Eric nodded and set off with his knights around him. He paired up the rest of the group into twos and selected Julie as his own scouting partner, suggesting to the others that he and Julie would take the farthest gate from the attack (and the least used in the city), noting,

"They could be sending another force to attack from that direction!"

As the knights charged off gallantly, and the rest of Tim's party went about to their assigned gates, the only one who gave Tim a suspicious look was Tink.

"See you soon, Tim," the little gnome said as he walked in step with the dwarf Ayers.

As soon as everyone was around the closest corner, Tim and Julie set off in a gallop towards the far city gate. The gate was named the North Gate for the obvious reason that it faced north, and even though it was an important trade access point, it was a rather small and unembellished structure. The city's streets were crawling with men, women, and children, all looking for a way to escape the doomed city.

Tim and Julie tried to stay as unnoticed as possible, but they found that a bit difficult with Julie's huge dog mount, who was growling and licking at any animal or child that got too close to them.

"Tim! Tim!"

The crowd began to cry as their newly elected hero appeared in their midst.

"No, no, not that Tim," Tim tried to say, but the crowd continued to close in around him and Julie, and Tim did not know what he could do.

Snapping his fingers, he rode his worthless donkey through the crowd and approached the closed gate. Tim got off his mount and looked to the gate. Standing with Shafty in his hand and applying a bit of a glow to the embedded gem in his… umm… shaft, the crowd parted around him. Tim shouted to the gate,

"We would really like to pass!"

He finished, and a bright gush of light shot forth from Shafty. The gatemen answered with silence. Tim looked over at Julie, who shrugged back at his master.

"We would really like to pass, please?" Tim said with equal enthusiasm.

A cackling laugh answered Tim this time. Tim took a step back at the sound and looked up to see a lithe form appear from the darkness.

"Hello, Tim. You look slightly less obese," she said with a whirring eyebrow. "Slavery must have suited you, though I find that incredibly surprising."

Tim looked down at his still-protruding belly and tried to arrange his robes in such a way that it made him look slightly less bulky.

"A lot of this is water weight, I'll have you know. It's from all my bulking in the arena," Tim said, padding himself all over.

Eliza laughed wickedly. Tim began to look around rather nervously.

"Anyway, Slagbottom—" Tim started, but this name drew a loud snicker from the crowd.

"Silence!" the witch snarled. The crowd went quiet, and all took a few steps back, leaving Tim to feel even more isolated.

"Well, Eliza, I don't really want to interrupt whatever it is you have planned for the city. So, if you wouldn't mind, would you be so kind as to open the gate and let myself and… and also these fine people go?" Tim said, gesturing broadly at the nearly panicked crowd.

He wiped the sweat off his profusely sweating brow and was extremely proud of how well he felt like he covered that. Eliza sauntered up to the side of the wall and looked down directly at Tim.

"No," she said simply, and before Tim could respond, she raised her hands into the air, and a magical gush of wind struck Tim and all of those standing around him.

Tim spat out the dirt that got caught in his mouth and couldn't help but think how terribly rude that was. I mean, it could be almost anything. Did Eliza even consider germs?

His thoughts of random bitchery quickly dispersed, however, when the large wooden doors swung inward. At first, he thought she had finally granted his request, but as the hulkish forms of undead guinea pog-looking beasts entered the city, Tim knew he was properly fucked.

"Zombie pogs!" Tim screeched, and the entire crowd

erupted into unbridled chaos at the sight of the undead monsters.

Tim could hear Eliza cackling with glee like a fat girl with cake as he blindly sprinted into the crowd. He lost Julie and Pig somewhere in the rolling tumult, but through it all, he could hear the wicked two-headed obsidian axes of the pogs sweeping into the screaming crowd.

Tim lost himself to the overwhelming fear of the hulking brutes. They were unnatural and a scourge from a dark god meant for darker times. He didn't know how he did it or how long it took him, but Tim found himself muddy, bloody, and tired, pawing at the large metal gate that was currently inhibiting his entry into the keep. After a few minutes, a guard recognized him and let the filthy wizard back into the castle. Tim was stunned, even with the ever-growing cascade of shit around him, that now there were chinchilladads tied up in the mix. That Eliza was a first-class cunt.

Tim found his way back to the wizard's tower and found Marlin and the queen trying to cope with rapidly changing circumstances. Most of the gates had now fallen, and several of the city's various quarters were considered lost and had been shut off from reinforcement. Slowly throughout the morning, most of Tim's companions filtered back into the command room, all looking just as broken as him.

Sir Eric was the first to arrive. His arm was clearly shattered and was tied closely to his torso with a white bandage; one of his eyes was soaked with blood, and he had a very strong limp.

"Sir Eric," Tim said, standing for the first time.

"Tim..." replied Eric, sounding morose.

"How fare the green knights?" Tim asked.

"It's both fitting and horrible that, as their commander,

I am the last of their number. The south gate was overrun with a mix of monsters. At first, we cut right through the rabble. I thought we were going to retake the gatehouse when the undead ones came. A horde of guinea pogs. They ate everything that lay before them, even the live and wounded of their allies. I... I... I couldn't..."

The knight tried to continue but broke down before he could finish.

"Sweet broccoli stalks!" Tim was actually beginning to think he was in real trouble.

Similar stories and similar stares greeted Tim as Tink, Leslie, and Ayers all joined, each with tales of woe and loss. Tim noticed that Aurora and Julie never made an appearance, and despite the very complicated relationship they all shared, Tim was worried — mostly for Aurora.

Julie was either stone-cold dead or was having the greatest day of his life out there. Tim wasn't sure which answer scared him more.

The map of the city continued to change throughout the day, and with the setting of the sun, the keep and its thick walls were the only thing remaining to the people of Myrmidon. It was full of refugees — as was the nearby sea. Anything that could float had more people than it could carry and was bobbing in the treacherous sea.

"What of Aurora?" Tim asked as the torches were beginning to be lit all around him.

The queen raised her head for the first time in what seemed like hours.

"Aurora? Has she not returned?" replied the queen.

Tim shook his head.

"Marlin!" the queen roared.

"What?" the mage yelled back.

Marlin had momentarily forgotten himself. Given the situation, most found it to be an acceptable trespass… this time.

"Are you aware my daughter is missing?"

Marlin looked cowed from his obvious lack of decorum in front of his queen.

"No, madam," he replied.

"Can you scry or use something else to find her?" Continued the queen.

"No, madam," the wizard said, lowering his head.

"Are you not said to be the most powerful wizard in the land?" the queen asked.

"Yes, madam," Marlin returned once again.

"Then forgive me, Marlin, but what exactly is the problem?" asked the queen agitatedly.

"The witch… she is somehow masking everything in the city. Only the castle and its walls are holding back her influence, but I fear that even that won't last long," Marlin explained.

The queen gave Marlin a curt look and addressed everyone in the now silent room.

"Ladies and Gentlemen, I will NOT lose this city," the queen stated with steel behind her words, making eye contact with as many people as possible. Then quietly, she said, "…and I will not lose my daughter. Can someone find her?"

Tim was leaning against a wall feeling just glum about Aurora. Though it would have taken him some time to get used to a normal female form, Tim thought he would have been able to make the transition as he looked around the palace at all the splendor. While this splendor was covered in blood at this particular time, it was still so nice. How would he ever become so rich? Tim wondered.

Then, as if by magic, Tim found himself stepping out from the wall and into the gathered crowd. It wasn't magic, of course; it was Shafty.

"Shafty!" Tim screamed mentally.

"Yes?" the long shaft asked.

"You're going to get me killed!" Tim cried in his mind.

The spear answered with a mental shrug and said,

"I'm just here to kill things, Tim."

"Oh, Tim… my hero!" the queen beamed and shot Marlin daggers with her glance.

Everyone else around him began to clap as well. Tim, not knowing how to refuse a queen, nodded and waved at everyone in the room and inwardly cursed Shafty's very soul to the deepest pits of hell.

"I, too, pledge my life and my sword, My Queen," Sir Eric said as he pulled out his bloodied green blade and kneeled with it.

"As the last of the green knights, no honor could be greater than dying with my men."

"You have always been a loyal knight, Eric. I expect you

to live or die by that," said the queen.

The green knight stood, nodded at his liege, and then walked over and stood by Tim.

"Aye, don't forget about us!" Ayers bellowed as he, Tink, Dick, and Leslie fought through the crowd. "Someone needs to watch these two's backs," the bloodied dwarf said, pointing at Tim and Eric. "If not, they'll likely die in a blaze of glory!"

Everyone thought it was great fun except Tim, who hated every moment of it.

The group did not have much of a set plan. Outside the castle, the entire city was overrun, so the general idea was to charge out the gates and then ride around a bit and look for the princess.

Sir Eric was able to recruit a few men at arms to serve as a vanguard force for the hero's party. Twenty men charged out on warhorses directly into the howling mass beyond the gate. In the chaos that followed, Tim's party slunk out the gate and headed in the opposite direction. It was amazing how much destruction the army of monsters had wrought in just a few hours. Bodies were strewn and half-eaten in the street. Shops and homes were burned, and the once great city of white stone and cedar was now a sooted ruin. The party rode up on a group of kobolds ripping apart a dead woman.

"Charge!" Eric bellowed and skewered the first kobold in his path.

Ayers was next and did a dwarven roll from his thick pony, cutting the legs off of a pair of the bunch. Leslie leapt from her saddle and plucked up one of the strange lizard dogs, headbutting it repeatedly. Two others ran off into the burning warrens of the city. Leslie laid out her prize and began to punch the little devil over and over.

"Leslie, what on earth are you doing?" Tim asked disgustedly.

"I wake up dog man," Leslie said.

"That's not how that works..." Tim started to say, but to his surprise, the little dog began to bark quietly.

"Now, dog man, speak," Leslie said and held it up by the scruff of his neck.

The little blue dog monster yipped and barked.

"Put me down, put me down, you great green..." he stopped for a minute and sniffed and then added a surprised, "...female?"

Leslie answered by shaking it violently.

"Stop, stop," the dog moaned. "First you burn home, then you kill us, now you torture us."

Luckily for Tim, everyone sort of glossed over this last part and Leslie barked back.

"Where is the princess, you little blue fuck?"

"Prin—" the dog started, but Leslie shook him again.

"At big mill house!" the dog yelped.

Leslie expertly snapped its neck and threw the dog to the ground.

"To the mill," the giant green she-beast said.

The party all dismounted and ran down the narrow cobbled streets, stopping to slay any kobolds that were too slow or too stupid to leave their path. Tim trotted in the back and looked for any chance to flee or something; he wasn't sure exactly.

Tim thought more than once he saw a giant dog moving behind the buildings or an impossibly sized pumpkin-shaped person. Before he could decide if it was Julie or not, the group burst out into the large plaza surrounding the huge ancient mill. In the middle of the square were huddled screaming women and children. All around them, kobolds launched in, tearing and ripping at the huddled mass. The party charged forth with even Tim losing himself in the moment. They cut, slashed, and burned their way to the women and children, and once they arrived, they realized they were too late. Most of the civilians were already dead, with just a few hanging on desperately to life. But the real trap was just springing into motion behind them: a wall of hooded chinchilladads and their guinea pog slaves formed an impossible square that was slowly moving closer to the small group. Dick looked up into the tower and shouted,

"It's Aurora!"

They all looked to see the bound princess dressed in white being marched out onto one of the large platforms surrounding the building. Standing right next to her was Eliza Slagbottom.

"Really, Tim? You hustled out of the safety of the castle for this?" she said, looking Aurora up and down.

"Even if you were the last man on earth and the second closest was a pig, she would go with the pig."

Shafty laughed in Tim's mind rather loudly.

"Er… hmm… let her go, Eliza!" Tim shouted back, sounding rather pathetic.

"No," she replied. "This is all your fault, Tim, all of it. Shall we recount the events for all your gathered friends here?" Eliza said.

Tim didn't answer and tried to not make eye contact with any of his friends.

"Some of you may know Tim and I went to school together. He was the fat, lazy, and stupid one, but he was a man. I was a hefty girl with an unfortunate facial structure and the butt of Tim's jokes. So, while he palled around and became a town wizard, I was sent to the far ends of the plains. On the way, my caravan was killed by goblins. They took me hostage and did whatever they wanted to me for years. Eventually my rage became physical, and I used my magic to destroy my sad clan of captors.

"Karen noticed this and welcomed me to the court of the undead. It was here that all my dreams were made real, and I was given the task to make the inner kingdoms perish for their treatment of me.

"One of our spies discovered a fat and stupid wizard was hoarding lost knowledge and was wasting it to scribble recipes. I knew at once it was you, fat oaf. So, we set to raid Halfass, but Tim was gone, as was his book. The little stunt on the bridge in the dwarven outpost lost me some time, but Tim and his book fell then into the hands of the kobolds.

"There, Tim's little sex slave… Julie? He began to barter with anyone in the underground and sold Tim's recipes one… at… a… time. I now have most of them," the witch said, holding up some sheets of paper.

"Unknown to Tim at the time, the pretty paper Julie collected for him was actually lost elven magic of extremely high value. But of course, Tim did figure this out before he fire-bombed the kobold city, displacing their population and setting the course for the city's destruction that we all see before us," Eliza said, gesturing all around her.

"Fucking dick," Eliza mumbled from up on the scaffold.

Tim kept his gaze on his shoes the entire time.

"…And to top it off, he just this morning requested his leave of the city to leave all of you to die in it."

Everyone looked hard at Tim.

"Which is a wish I will grant," Eliza said, and she started to cast.

As Eliza's hands began to trace the intricate weave with her delicate fingers, the light slowly began to leave the world around them. Storm clouds appeared from nowhere, billowing and bulging around the powerful witch, and a dark rain began to fall. The group could hear Eliza mumbling, but only Shafty's keen telepathic ear knew the actual words.

"Tim, Tim, TIM!" the spear shouted. "Throw me with haste!"

Tim, just wanting the spear to be quiet, took Shafty from his back and hurled him into the nearby stream.

"Fucking mor—" the spear started as it disappeared beneath the churning water below.

Eliza continued to cast, and even through the conjured darkness, Tim could see her beginning to sweat. At a high point, she let out a scream and collapsed to the wooden platform.

"Hooray!" Tim cheered and looked around at all of his friends.

No one was smiling. Tim was about to try again when the earth all around them began to shake. Tim was not sure what to call the thing that emerged before him. A sea-man monster?

The churning dark waters of Myrmidon were now becoming

awash in the shattering flotsam of the refugees and their cob-
bled-together life rafts. Dozens died as the hulking, ropey being
of the deep rose to its full and terrifying height of a hundred
and fifty feet. The ancient mill tower, one of the tallest buildings
in the proud old city, was dwarfed by its cyclopean magnitude.
Tim was truly dumbstruck.

Looking even more closely, Tim could see hundreds, no thousands, no tens of thousands of baby sea turtle skeletons? Gods,
why did Eliza have to suck so much? The great monster swung
its clawed hand and scooped up another wave of innocents.
Some were eaten; some were hurled to their deaths much deeper into the city.

Tim didn't have time to think; he just reacted. Looking over to
his friends, he shouted,

"Save Aurora!" then began running to the docks.

Holding out his hand, he summoned Shafty from the depths.

"I knew you could run—" Shafty started.

"Not right now!" Tim screamed as he increased his speed
and made his way down to the frothing waterway below.

Still running on pure instinct, Tim shot forth a more moderately
sized fireball, unlike the Armageddon variety he had unleashed
on the kobolds. The substantial ball struck the sea beast in its
torso and caused the great hulk to take a single step back.

Reaching the end of the dock, again not thinking, Tim extended Shafty, and the pair flew up, up, and away. Instead of fire,
as he leapt, he imagined his own little twist on a classic flambé
recipe—he had been saving it for a special occasion when some
woman or another would have come and stayed over at Kim.
That never happened, so he had never bothered with it. The recipe page was clear in his mind, however, and the magic began
to form through him.

Instead of lighting the dessert on fire, like any idiot, Tim's plan was to conjure a bit of electricity into the mix to razzle and dazzle his guests. This somehow felt even better.

Great balls and strands of lightning began to shoot from his hands and the extended weapon of war. The electric onslaught released a tremendous thunderclap as he blew a hole clear through the thick chest of the summoned monstrosity. Shafty and Tim rode the wave straight through the monster and out the other side.

Shafty shouted with glee the entire time.

"Yippeeeeeee!"

As they exited the monster's chest, Shafty self-corrected, raising his tip from six to midnight so they could circle around for another pass. The duo rounded the monster's head, and just as they flew by, a hand the size of a house struck them, rocketing Tim into the city far below.

*T*he next thing Tim knew, he was sitting, well lying, in what used to be a small bakery shop. It appeared Tim had landed where they stored the fresh eggs. He had egg all over his face.

"Great," Tim said dejectedly and called out for Shafty.

No answer.

Walking out into the streets, Tim found himself in a daze and saw what seemed to be a city returning to normal all around him. Soldiers were piling the corpses of guinea pogs, kobolds, and the odd chinchilla, stacking them deep onto a four-wheeled cart. People were generally going around and picking up what remained of their town and their lives.

As a young boy ran by, Tim reached out and stopped him.

"Young lad, what day is it? What happened?" Tim asked.

The boy looked at Tim for a second before answering.

"I know you…" the boy started, then continued, "Marlin saved us all from the monster, and the dark army retreated; we are saved!" he said and ran off towards the busied guards.

"Marlin? What the hell did he do? I was the one who—" Tim stopped as the two guards approached him with steel drawn.

"Tim?" they asked.

"Yes," Tim answered happily; he was their hero after all.

The two guards looked Tim over, and without saying a word, the one on the left knocked his lights out. Tim was asleep again.

197

*T*im awoke for the second time that day after an un-ceremonious shot to his brain pan. This time, he found himself wearing a dirty cloth shirt and pants and found his hands heavi-ly manacled as he was being dragged across the floor of the palace.

Tim tried to speak but found he was gagged. Still gathering his wits, he was carried and dragged to the throne room where the queen sat in court. She looked pissed. As did Aurora, Marlin, Ayers, Leslie, Eric, and Dick, along with every still-living noble in Myrmidon.

Tim mumbled through his gag.

"Ah, what was that, Tim the Traitor?" Marlin asked.

"That's a magical gag, you see. We can't have you conjur-ing your way out of this one."

"Oh fudge," Tim mumbled through his gag.

No one could hear him. The queen stood and stared at Tim long and hard.

"For betraying this kingdom, my daughter and I, Queen Vagimite, hereby condemn you to a life of hard labor. This will not be over quickly. There's a city to be rebuilt, and you and your back will do as much of it as wizardly possible. My kingdom is in shambles, rogue armies now swarm the fields of Myrmidon, and the worst kind of magic is loose in the hands of monsters everywhere. You will not see the end of this, Tim," the queen proclaimed.

Tim sighed. He wasn't going to be able to sit, eat, or nap again for a very long time.

As Tim sat there listening to his judgment, a page entered the room, whispered something in Marlin's ear, and handed him a sealed scroll. Marlin then whispered to the queen, and the two held a private audience — with Marlin casting a privacy spell so that they could not be overheard. At the end of it, the queen excused herself, and Marlin approached the bound and gagged prisoner. He whispered so only the terrified Tim could hear.

"Well, Tim, it seems your troubles have traveled farther than you could have ever imagined, and for that, the punishment must fit the crime. Enjoy what very well might be your last night in Myrmidon, for it will be the last one you rest in this world or any other," the old wizard said, mischievously grinning with a curious twinkle in his eye.

Tim gulped.

Epilogue

*A*s Julie waited for nightfall, he approached the floating debris of the now dead sea monster.

A small, plump four-fingered hand reached out as a shard of pure darkness left the monster's carcass and entered into Julie.

Like recognizes like.